W9-BNZ-028

The Mistletoe Secret

Center Point
Large Print

Also by Richard Paul Evans and available
from Center Point Large Print:

The Mistletoe Collection
  The Mistletoe Promise
  The Mistletoe Inn
The Walk Series
  A Step of Faith
  Walking on Water

**This Large Print Book carries the
Seal of Approval of N.A.V.H.**

The Mistletoe Secret

RICHARD PAUL EVANS

CENTER POINT LARGE PRINT
THORNDIKE, MAINE

BOCA RATON PUBLIC LIBRARY
BOCA RATON, FLORIDA

This Center Point Large Print edition is published
in the year 2017 by arrangement with
Simon & Schuster, Inc.

Copyright © 2016 by Richard Paul Evans.

All rights reserved.

This book is a work of fiction. Any references to
historical events, real people, or real places are used
fictitiously. Other names, characters, places, and events
are products of the author's imagination, and any
resemblance to actual events or places or persons,
living or dead, is entirely coincidental.

The text of this Large Print edition is unabridged.
In other aspects, this book may vary
from the original edition.
Printed in the United States of America
on permanent paper.
Set in 16-point Times New Roman type.

ISBN: 978-1-68324-225-3

Library of Congress Cataloging-in-Publication Data

Names: Evans, Richard Paul, author.
Title: The mistletoe secret / Richard Paul Evans.
Description: Center Point Large Print edition. | Thorndike, Maine :
Center Point Large Print, 2017.
Identifiers: LCCN 2016043653 | ISBN 9781683242253
    (hardcover : alk. paper)
Subjects: LCSH: Large type books. | Christmas stories. | GSAFD:
Love stories.
Classification: LCC PS3555.V259 M575 2017 | DDC 813/.54—dc23
LC record available at https://lccn.loc.gov/2016043653

BOCA RATON PUBLIC LIBRARY
BOCA RATON, FLORIDA

To Trish Todd
With gratitude for your boundless patience.
It's been a pleasure working with you.

Prologue

Aria winced as she picked up a half-eaten rice-paper egg roll that someone had smashed into the table's crystal centerpiece. "Really? Would you do that at your own home?" she mumbled to herself, then dropped the roll into the tub she was busing the table with. The diner she worked at occasion-ally catered weddings, and in a town as small as Midway, Aria always knew someone at the wedding—usually the bride or groom, if not both. At tonight's celebration the bride, Charise, was her boss's niece.

The bride had looked beautiful in her lace-topped, ivory satin dress. Beautiful *and* happy. Aria scolded herself for wondering how long it would last.

She remembered her own wedding day and the beautiful dress she'd had to sell three months ago to make rent after her Jeep's alternator went out. Even though it hadn't been much of a wedding, not even by a small town's standards, she had been happy then too. She had the pictures to prove it. But there had been cracks in the façade of nuptial bliss. Her groom, Wade, had been controlling and short-tempered and shouted at her just a half hour before the wedding ceremony, berating her for inviting someone he didn't like to the wedding. He had also drunk a lot and embarrassed the few people who actually showed up to the party. She remembered fearing that she'd made a mistake, a fear she quickly brushed away with thoughts of her alternative option—embarrassment, loneliness, and living with her mother.

All the same, her fear had been right. Just a few years after the ceremony, Wade left her stranded —alone and broke in a small, Swiss-style town out west, far from her home in Minnesota. And tonight she was picking up the mess of someone else's wedding before going home alone. She tried to ignore the painful inner voices that chided her. If she never made it home, would anyone really care? Would it be this way the rest of her life? And the biggest question of all: Is anyone else out there?

Chapter
One

Whether we admit it or not, most of us live our lives on autopilot. We wake at the same hour, go to the same place of work or worship, talk to the same people, eat at the same restaurants, even watch the same TV shows. I'm not criticizing this. Habit is stability and stability is vital to survival. There's a reason farmers don't change crops mid-season. When wisdom does not require change, it is wisdom not to change.

But sometimes the evolving terrain of life requires us to evolve with it. When those times come, we usually find ourselves quivering on the precipice of change as long as we can, because no one wants to dive headlong into the ravine of uncertainty. No one. Only when the pain of being becomes too much do we close our eyes and leap.

This is the story of my jump—a time when I did one of the most bizarre things I've ever done: I hunted down a woman I didn't know, in a small town I'd never heard of, just because of something she posted on the Internet.

I've heard it said that solitude is among the greatest of all suffering. It's true, I think. Humans don't do well alone. But it's not really solitude that's the problem—it's loneliness. The difference between solitude and loneliness is that one exists in the physical world, and the other exists in the heart. A person can be in solitude but not lonely, and vice versa. My job has taken me to some of the most crowded cities in the world and I've still seen and felt loneliness. I've seen it in the cold spaces between strangers jostling next to one another on the crowded sidewalks. I've heard it in a thousand rushed conversations. We have more access to humanity than ever before and less connection.

I'm not a stranger to loneliness. It was part of my childhood. There was loneliness between my mother and father. They never divorced. I think they stayed together because they didn't want to be alone, but they were terribly lonely. And terribly unhappy. By the time I was sixteen I promised myself that if I ever got married, my marriage would be different. Ah, the best-laid plans.

My name is Alex Bartlett. Bartlett like the pear. If I had to pick a starting point for when my story began, it was this time last year, approaching the holidays.

I live and work in Daytona Beach, Florida, a town made famous by fast cars and smooth beaches. I have one of those unromantic jobs with a company you've never heard of, doing something you've never thought about and never would have if I didn't tell you about it. I work for a company called Traffix. We sell traffic management systems for transportation departments. Basically, the product I sell counts the vehicles on the freeway and then sends in traffic analyses. If you've ever seen one of those electric freeway signs that tell you how many minutes to the airport, that's probably my company's software doing the calculating. I don't design it. I just sell it.

My sales territory was in the US Northwest, which includes Northern California, Oregon, and Washington State. Since I live on the East Coast, that meant I traveled a lot for work, sometimes for stretches of weeks. I hated the loneliness of the road and being gone from home. My wife, Jill, hated my traveling too. But only at first. After a few years, she got used to it and took to creating a life without me. It seemed that every time I came home, reentry was more difficult. After five years she seemed indifferent to my traveling. I was lonely at home as well.

Believing that my absence was hurting our marriage, I took a pay cut and traveled less. But as soon as I started spending more time at home, I realized that things had changed more than I realized. At least Jill had. She was different. She seemed uninterested in us—or maybe just me. She had become secretive.

Then she started traveling with a group of

women she met online. At least that's what she told me she was doing. One day I was helping out with the laundry while she was gone and I found a folded-up, handwritten note in her jeans.

My deer one,

Each day were apart from each other feels like years. Your so far away. Im sorry that I couldnt come with you this time. I cant bear the idea of loosing you. I cant wate until you return and we will feest again on each others love.

—Your Clark

A sick, paralyzing fear went through my body. My face flushed red and my hands began to tremble. The idiot couldn't even spell. But idiot or not he had my wife. When I had calmed down enough to speak I called Jill.

"Who's Clark?" I asked.

There was a long pause. "Clark? Why?"

"Tell me who he is."

"I have no idea what you're talking about."

"I found a note from him in your jeans."

She hesitated for a moment, then said, "Oh, right. He's Katherine's lover. She handed that note to me as we got off the Phoenix flight so her husband didn't find it. It's nothing. I mean, to Katherine it's something, she wanted me to hold on to it, but it has nothing to do with me."

I just sat there processing her excuse. The fact that Jill's name wasn't on the note left me little ground to dispute her claim, even though it seemed unlikely. "You're not cheating on me?"

"Why would I cheat on you?"

"But Katherine's cheating on her husband."

"Yes. And I can't say that I blame her. She's been going to divorce him for, like, two years, she's just waiting for the right time. He's got a bunch of real estate deals pending and she doesn't want to throw a divorce on top of that."

"Thoughtful of her," I said sarcastically.

"She's not doing it for him," she said, apparently missing my sarcasm. "If these sales go through, she'll make a boatload in the divorce. Why would you think I was cheating on you?"

I wasn't sure how to answer. "You're gone a lot lately."

"You've been gone most of our marriage. I never assumed you were cheating."

I honestly didn't know if I should feel more foolish for doubting her or for believing her. I finally just breathed out slowly. "All right. Be safe. I miss you."

"I miss you too. 'Bye."

We were together only five days after she returned before I left town on business to Tacoma. A week later I came home to an empty house and a note on the kitchen table.

Dear Alex,

There is a season for all things and it is my season to spread my wings and fly. I can no longer be held inside this cage, gilded though it may be, like a sad, lonely bird. I cannot bear the thought of someday looking back with regret over what might have been.

It's not you, Alex, at least it hasn't been your intent to keep me so unhappy. You are a kind soul. It's me and the human spirit yearning to fly. I need to be free and freedom cannot be contained within the shackles of a loveless marriage. I wish you to find freedom and love as well.

Sincerely,
Jill

P.S. I took the money from our savings and 401k.

She needed to be "free?" She was already free to do whatever she wanted, wherever and whenever she wanted. It was painful not understanding, not knowing what she meant, other than not wanting to be attached to me.

A few weeks later, pictures surfaced online of my ex-wife with another man. She wasn't traveling with "just the girls" as she had claimed. I saw a picture of Clark with his arm around my wife. He looked like a cross between a young Tom Selleck and a mandrill monkey. I felt like such an idiot for missing her secrets and believing her lies. Especially for believing her lies. The lies hurt more than her betrayal. Anyone can have their head turned, but the lies were continual evidence that she didn't love me. She hadn't for a very long time. Maybe she never had.

I vowed that I would never let someone lie to me again.

Now that she was gone I was just as alone as when I had been married, only now it was official. Some of us, maybe most of us, are good at attracting what we claim we don't want. My life seemed doomed to loneliness.

Chapter Two

It was the Friday evening before Thanksgiving and I was still at work. Half the office lights were off and, except for the janitorial staff, I hadn't seen anyone in the building for several hours. I didn't really need to work late, I just didn't have anywhere else to be and going home to an empty apartment was the last thing I wanted to do.

A little after eight, I heard footsteps shuffling toward me. I looked up to see Nate, one of my co-workers, leaning against his cane and holding out an unopened can of Red Bull. "Here, man. Just what every insomniac needs for dinner."

I took the can from him and popped its tab. "Thanks."

"How's it going?"

"It's going."

I had worked with Nate for about three and a half years in the sales department, and during that time he'd become more friend than co-worker. I'd always thought that Nate didn't look like a salesman. He was a scary-looking guy— "formidable," one of our managers once called him. He was as bald as a thumb, with a long blond beard that forked like a snake's tongue. His biceps and forearms, which were massive, were covered in tattoos. At one time he could bench-press more than four hundred fifty pounds—roughly two and a half of me.

Before coming to Traffix, Nate had been a Marine. If you asked him, he would tell you that he was still a Marine. Once a Marine, *always* a Marine. Between Operation Desert Shield and Desert Storm, Nate had seen a lot of action and a lot of bad things. He still suffered from PTSD. One time his wife woke in the night to find Nate crawling around the room on his elbows and knees, dodging enemy fire.

He left the marines after surviving his second IED explosion, in which he'd lost all of his teeth, broken his back, and partially lost his sense of balance. Even broken up as he was, he was still the toughest person I'd ever met.

Nate had good stories, and by "good" I mean interesting to listen to, which he rarely shared and only with the few people he trusted. But when he did, they practically erupted out of him, as if they'd been building up pressure just waiting to burst out.

Once, about a year after he left the marines, Nate was at a gun expo and stopped at a vendor's booth to admire a hunting rifle. "This for deer?" he asked.

The proprietor looked at him with a condescending smile. "Of course. What's the matter, haven't you ever hunted before?"

Without flinching, Nate looked him in the eyes and said softly, "Not animals."

The man's smile disappeared.

"What are you still doing here?" I asked.

"That's what I was going to ask you," Nate said. He pulled a chair out from the cubicle across from me and sat, resting his cane between his legs. "I just landed. I wanted to input the sale before I went home."

"Where have you been?"

"St. Louis. Finally closed it."

"Congrats."

"Thanks. That bonus check will be the down payment on my Christmas present to myself this year. My new truck. Unless Ashley takes it." He smiled slightly. "So what's your excuse?"

"No place else to be."

"Have you had dinner?"

"No."

He stood. "Let's get some man food. And by that I mean beer." As I closed out my computer Nate said, "I'm calling Dale to meet us."

Dale was another salesman at Traffix. His region was the mirror opposite of mine: East Coast, the New England area. He was shorter than me by at least six inches and looked a little like Michael Keaton when he wore his wire-rimmed glasses.

Dale was also the self-proclaimed, designated

wisecracking comic relief that every man-pack requires. Really, the guy lived in a mental bounce house. Sometimes being around him seemed like more work than it was worth, but he was a good guy and always lightened things up.

I drove Nate to our usual haunt, The Surly Wench Pub & Café. We had been going to this place for years, even back when it had different management and a different name: The Pour House. The new name was more fitting for its new proprietor.

Dale was already seated at a table when we arrived. Being a weekend night, the pub was crowded and the noise level was only slightly lower than a chain saw demonstration. There were three mugs of beer in front of Dale, one of them a quarter down.

"Ahoy, me maties," Dale said in a pirate voice. "Join me in a grog."

"Why are you talking like that?" Nate asked, sitting down.

"Arrr, doncha know what day it be?"

"Day to talk like an idiot?"

"No, you filthy bilge rat. It be International Talk Like a Pirate Day."

Nate took a drink, then said, "There's no such thing."

"Aye, that's whar you'd be wrong, matie."

"Stop that," Nate said.

Dale turned to me. "What be going on, you landlubber? Nate said it be arrrr-gent."

21

"Nate closed St. Louis."

"Aye," Dale said, lifting his mug. "Thar be reason for a celebratin'!"

Nate pointed a finger at him. "If you keep talking like that, I swear I will rip out your tongue and strangle you with it."

Dale, who was something like half Nate's size or, at least, muscle mass, cleared his throat. "All right," he said, resuming his normal voice. "As you wish."

"Thank you," Nate said. "And we're not here to celebrate my sale. We're here to talk about Alex's woman problem."

Dale set down his drink. "Argh. Tales of the filthy wench."

Nate pointed at him again and Dale lifted his hands in surrender. "All right, you and your steroidal biceps win." He turned back to me. "Nate's right, my man. You've got to get over her. It's been a year."

"Eleven months."

"Close enough," Nate said. "Really. It's time to stop grieving your marriage's corpse. It's time to just bite the bullet."

"I'd rather put one through my head."

Dale glanced at Nate. "That's not good."

Nate took a long drink of his beer and then leaned in close. "Let me ask you something. If Jill called you tonight and asked you to come back, would you?"

I thought for a moment, then said, "Yeah. I probably would."

He shook his head. "I was afraid of that."

"What's wrong with forgiveness?" I asked.

"To err is human, to forgive is divine. Neither is Marine Corps policy." He took a drink, then said, "Jill was sucking the life out of you long before she cheated on you. Why are you looking for happiness where you lost it?"

"We always look for things where we lost them. Keys, wallets, sunglasses."

"He's got a point," Dale said.

Nate frowned. "Just be grateful there aren't kids involved. She'd use them as human shields."

"She's not that bad."

"Since when is she not that bad?"

Nate was right. "So how does one 'bite the bullet'?"

"You burn the bridges, sink the boats. You cross the Rubicon."

Dale started in. "In non-Marine jargon, it means you leave the past behind and start living your future. It's time to find someone new. You're a good-looking guy, successful, smart—there's a million women out there who would love to hook up with you."

"They're pounding down my doors," I said.

"They would be if they knew you were available," Nate said. "It's like this: you don't stop someone in a parking lot to ask if their car's for

23

sale unless it has a sign in the window. You need to put up the sign."

"You want me to wear a sign saying I'm single?"

"Figuratively," Nate said.

"He could get a T-shirt," Dale interjected. "Available."

Nate continued. "I could name at least a half dozen women at Traffix who would be interested."

"You think I should date someone at work?"

"Absolutely not. I'm just saying there're opportunities out there."

Just then our waitress, Corinne, brought over a tray of cheeseburger sliders, buffalo wings, and spinach artichoke dip with tortilla chips. "There you go, my darlings."

"Avast, me buxom beauty," Dale said. "Now give us a twirl and show us your aftside."

She shook her head. "What's wrong with him?"

"It's Talk Like a Pirate Day," I said.

"That must be why the kitchen's all talking like that." She turned to me. "Where have you been, dear?"

"Hiding," I said.

"Men usually come *here* to hide."

"Woman problems," Nate said.

"That's usually why they're hiding." She smiled at me. "Need another drink?"

"He could use a keg," Nate said.

"Keep 'em a-comin, ya wench," Dale said.

24

"And don't go a-hornswoggling us on the bill."

Corinne shook her head, then looked back at me. "For the record, I'm available." She winked and walked back to the kitchen.

"There you have it," Nate said. "Opportunity."

"The hurt's still fresh," I said. "I'm not looking for *opportunity*."

"Don't you miss waking up to something soft and warm in bed?" Dale asked. "Be truthful, aren't you lonely?"

I took a slow drink, then nodded. "Yeah. Sometimes it feels like the flu."

Both men looked at me sympathetically.

"Your situation isn't going to change by itself," Nate said. "You've got to make the world change. If you're looking for something, where do you go?"

"Looking for what?"

"Anything. A new stereo system. A book."

"I'd probably look it up on the Internet."

"Bingo. That's where you start."

"You think I should try Internet dating?"

"At least in the beginning," Nate said.

"I've heard bad stories about Internet dating."

"All dating has bad stories. Big deal. So you have to sift through a few tares to get to the wheat."

"What's a tare?" Dale asked.

"It's a weed," Nate said. "Don't you ever read the Bible?"

Dale shook his head. "Not enough, apparently."

25

He turned to me. "I know it doesn't sound fun, but sometimes you have to go through hell to get to heaven. Do you know Wally in engineering? The short guy with a bad haircut?"

"The guy with a big handlebar mustache that makes him look like a walrus?"

"That's the man," Dale said, touching his nose as if we were playing charades. "So, three years ago he was married to this demon shrew who was as bossy as she was lazy. He's working his butt off to pay bills, while she stays at home during the day shopping for junk jewelry on TV and eating chocolate, you know what I mean?" He didn't wait for me to answer.

"After their youngest kid starts school, the shrew makes friends with a group of younger students and starts staying up all night clubbing. Then she stops getting out of bed in the morning because she's too tired from staying up so late, so Wally starts getting up at five in the morning so he can make the kids' lunches and breakfasts, send them off to school, and go to work.

"But it doesn't end there. Her enlightened friends convince her that she's a domestic slave, so she claims herself 'emancipated' from Wally, which means she officially doesn't have to do anything other than cash his checks and spend his money.

"So every day after work the man comes home, makes dinner, does the dishes, puts the kids to

26

bed, then goes to bed himself to start again the next day. I mean, it's an insane arrangement, but Wally's a timid, peaceful soul and he does this without complaint.

"This goes on for more than a year. Then one day the demon shrew tells him that he's boring and ugly and she wants a divorce. He pleads with her to stay because of the children, but she's not having it. So she drains their savings and takes off with her buddies and the guy she was secretly seeing."

"This sounds kind of familiar," I said.

"Too familiar," Nate said.

"So, the divorce goes through and it wreaks havoc on the kids. They start getting in fights and getting expelled from school, that kind of stuff. Still, Wally does his best to be both parents, since the ex never has time to see her kids anymore.

"Then, about three months after the divorce is final, Marco in engineering comes up to Wally and says, 'Aren't you divorced?' Wally says, 'Yeah, why do you ask?' Marco tells him that his wife's sister is coming up from Mexico and even though she doesn't speak much English, she's sweet and pretty and not married. He invites Wally on a double date.

"Wally asks, 'Why me?' Marco says, 'Why not you? You're a nice guy.' So Wally shows up at Marco's house and it turns out that his sister-in-law isn't just pretty, she's gorgeous. Like, *drop-*

dead gorgeous. I mean, on a scale of one to ten she's pushing fifty, and here's Wally on a good hair day pushing four. Love must be blind because Martina, that's her name, is smitten. She barely speaks English, but they speak the language of love. They start dating.

"One night she asks if they can stay home. Martina makes Wally a real home-cooked Mexican meal, then afterward, she tells him to just relax in the living room. She brings him a cold drink and turns the TV on for him, then—get this—gets down on her knees and rubs his feet. He doesn't know how to handle it.

"Six months later, they get married. One day Martina comes to him crying. Wally asks her what's wrong. She says, 'My love, you are so handsome. I know you have many beautiful women who want you. I am afraid one will come and take you from me.'

"Wally says, 'No one is going to take me. No one thinks I'm handsome but you.' She says, 'You are humble too. I will never be able to hold you.'

"Karma," Dale said, leaning back in emphasis. "Sometimes the route to heaven goes through hell. Karma may pay slow, but she eventually covers the bill."

"Where did you hear this story?" I asked.

"Marco. Martina came down to bring Wally lunch and I asked him who the looker was."

Nate raised his glass to me. "Dale's right, man.

Heaven awaits. You just need to apply yourself. It's like Stuart always says in sales conference, 'Nothings sells itself.' "

I took another drink and then said, "The Internet, huh?"

Dale nodded. "You can find whatever you want on the Internet."

"Give it a try," Nate said. "There's a dating site for everyone."

I thought for a moment, then said, "All right."

Nate looked at me seriously. " 'All right,' you'll do it, or 'all right,' you've said your piece, now leave me alone?"

"The former," I said. "I'll try."

"Try not," Dale said in a pitched voice. "Do, or do not."

"You sound like Yoda."

"I was imitating him."

"I prefer the pirate."

"Aye, then. Make us proud, matie," Dale said. "Scuttle ye boats."

"Scuttle ye boats," Nate said.

"Scuttle ye boats," I repeated.

We all took a drink.

Chapter
Three

We stayed at the pub until a little after eleven, when Dale's wife, Michelle, called to see where he was. From Dale's end of the conversation we could tell she wasn't happy.

"You really left Michelle alone on a Friday night and didn't tell her where you were going?" Nate said as Dale hung up.

"Slipped my mind."

"Keep that up," Nate said, "and *you're* going to be Internet dating."

"No, she'll just give me the silent treatment for a few days, which is kind of like a staycation. That reminds me. The other day Michelle asked me to hand her the lip balm but I accidentally handed her the superglue instead. She's still not speaking to me."

I laughed.

"Good one, Dale," Nate said. "Good one."

I picked up the tab, gave Nate a lift back to his car, then drove home to my apartment. Even though it was past midnight, I turned on the television. I watched the last twenty minutes of *Citizen Kane*, then began surfing channels.

Just as I was about to turn off the television, an advertisement came on for a dating site—a video collage of happy, love-frenzied couples swooning over each other. It seemed to me like some kind of a sign. I took a deep breath and got up from the couch. "All right, fine. Let's do this."

I walked over to my computer and pulled up the dating site advertised on the commercial. The home page showed an attractive couple laughing, their faces touching, their eyes blissfully closed.

LONELINESS OR LOVE?
It's your choice with eDate.

As I looked at the page a pop-up box appeared.

Tell us, are you:

  a) A man seeking a woman
  b) A woman seeking a man
  c) A man seeking a man
  d) A woman seeking a woman
  e) Other

Other? I clicked "a," then entered my zip code and country. The box disappeared and three words appeared:

Let's Go, Stud.

Interesting beginning. I wondered what it said to women.

I started answering questions. There were a lot

of them. I hadn't realized that signing up for a dating site would be like taking an SAT exam, but the site advertised the proven power of its matching process, and if true love was at the end of it all, it was a small price to pay.

I clicked through the basic questions, answering them as quickly as possible. Gender, age, city, relationship status—single or divorced. One of the prompts asked me how many times I'd been married; the options started at zero and went all the way up to five-plus. *Who goes after people that have been married five-plus times?* I wondered. Probably other people who have been married five-plus times. They should get a frequent marriage card.

In the next segment, I was asked to rate my own personality traits on a scale of one to five. Was I warm? Clever? Sensitive? Generous? After a while I just started marking fours for everything until the website scolded me.

Slow down, partner. We know you're excited, but you're answering too many questions the same. Take time to carefully consider and answer each question. Your future happiness is at stake.

So much at stake. I threw in some threes and fives, not necessarily because I thought it was more accurate, but rather just to please the software. After ten minutes of questions, I clicked FINISHED. The site congratulated me for not quitting, and then a graph popped up showing that I was only 10 percent done. "Ten percent?" I said to myself. This was going to take all night.

The third segment asked more questions along the personality line and I was asked to pick out adjectives that described me:

Content
Genuine
Vivacious
Wise
Bossy
Aggressive
Opinionated
Romantic

Are people actually honest on these sites? Do people actually choose people who admit to being bossy, aggressive, and opinionated? So far the site hadn't asked if I had a police record or if I'd ever been accused of a felony. Maybe that came later.

The questions continued. It was annoyingly long, sometimes asking the same question in a different way, presumably to trick liars into revealing themselves. There were a lot of questions I should have asked Jill before marrying her. But then, the Jill who divorced me wasn't the same person

I'd married anyway. If you think about it, when you marry someone, you're just jumping into one part of a very long river, hoping the current takes you somewhere worthwhile.

Then again, maybe she would have just lied anyway; she was good at it.

After the fifth segment I was informed by the graph that I was only halfway done. It was half past one in the morning and I was tired of answering questions, but now I felt trapped, unwilling to throw away all my work. I reminded myself of how lonely I was and that I'd had a Red Bull along with my beers. There was no turning back.

The ninth segment asked me what I did for a living. I wrote *consultant,* which, in a matter of speaking, was true, but mostly just sounded better than saying I was a salesman. Still, it made me feel a little sneaky.

The next segment asked me to rate my looks, then post pictures of myself. I suppose that it's somewhat revealing that I didn't have any pictures that didn't have Jill in them. I'm not a "selfie" kind of guy, but I snapped a picture of myself and uploaded it.

By experience, I know that most women think I'm attractive, but I'm not vain and the selfie I took should have proved it, easily dropping me a few points on the *Hot or Not* scale. At least no one would accuse me of Photoshopping my profile pic. That was my professional slogan: under-promise, overdeliver.

When I finally reached the end of the survey I was asked which of the service's packages I wished to purchase. I got out my credit card and paid for ninety days of the gold package, the highest level possible.

Okay, I did it, I thought. *The trap is set.*

Sometimes the most profound experiences of our lives start with an act so simple and careless that we hardly think about it—like tossing a small stone that causes a massive avalanche. I don't know what possessed me, maybe it was the beer or the hour, but, on a whim, I typed "lonely" into a search engine and scrolled through a few pages of mostly song lyrics before landing on a blog post with the title "Is Anyone Out There?"

I clicked on the link, which took me to a blog site with the initials LBH at the top. There was a silhouette of a woman, but her face was indistinguishable.

Is Anyone Out There?

Dear Universe,

I'm so lonely tonight it hurts. Is anyone out there? Can you hear me? I once heard it said that the Internet is like a dark hallway you shout down—you don't know if anyone is there.

So here's the existential question of the day. If you blog something and nobody reads it, did you make a sound?
Sigh.

—LBH

I looked at the navigation bar for a profile or an *about me* page but there wasn't one. Whoever this woman was, she wasn't particularly interested in being identified. Just initials. LBH.

I scrolled down and read the previous blog entries she had posted, reading from the most recent back to the beginning.

Dear Universe,
This morning I was walking in to work from my car and looked up to see a single orange balloon floating into the sky. I was late for work but something made me stop and watch it get smaller and smaller, until it disappeared into the clouds. I guess I felt like it needed a witness, someone to stand there and say *I saw you float away. I saw you disappear.* I wish someone would do that for me.

—LBH

Dear Universe,
Many great minds and people have addressed loneliness. In *East of Eden,*

John Steinbeck wrote, "All great and precious things are lonely." Mother Teresa said, "The most terrible poverty is loneliness, and the feeling of being unloved." Norman Cousins wrote, "The eternal quest of the individual human being is to shatter his loneliness."

I don't know that I'm adding anything with these little blog posts, but the thought that someone might read them somehow makes me feel less alone. If you're reading this, Thank you. If you're not, don't tell me.

—LBH

Dear Universe,

Why do we consider loneliness to be so shameful? A recent study showed that we are not alone in our loneliness. A full 40 percent of adults described themselves as being lonely. Yet people go to great lengths to make it appear as if they are *not* lonely. I recently read an interview where a top loneliness researcher sat reading a copy of his own book in public (a self-help book with the word *lonely* in the title) and suddenly became very embarrassed. What if the people around him noticed the book and thought he was lonely? His thought surprised him. Why was it that he, someone who studied loneliness for a living and therefore *knows* how pervasive it is, was so afraid of being perceived as lonely?

I have a theory. Perhaps we're afraid our loneliness will make us appear less lovable, less attractive, and less worthy of connection, and therefore more lonely.

Ironically, I'm not alone in my loneliness. Maybe that's why I keep these posts anonymous. We want to be lovable. We don't want to be alone. So we hide our loneliness, and it makes us . . . well . . . lonely.

—LBH

Dear Universe,

Okay, here's something that concerns you, dear reader. Did you know that the amount of time you spend online is inversely related to your general state of happiness and connection? In other words, the more time you spend online, the more unhappy and isolated you feel. I know that doesn't put either of us in a very good position, seeing as we are both online right now. But have you ever taken the time to think about why we spend so much time online? Why the average adult checks their social media upward of seventeen times a day?

I think that, misguided as it is, we *are* trying to connect. It's just that we don't know how, and maybe we can't stop ourselves from trying in this way. I know that the answer to my loneliness won't be found on a computer screen. And yet here I am. Reaching out. I wish I knew if anyone was reading this.

—LBH

Dear Universe,

Tonight I'm trying something new. I heard a psychiatrist talking on the radio. She said that writing out our feelings can not only help us understand ourselves, but can help take the pain from us. So here I go with my own experiment. Starting tonight I will begin the task of chronicling the life of a lonely woman. A woman who desperately wants to love and to be loved. I don't know if anyone will ever read this except me and God, but I'm trusting the psychiatrist. At least for now. It's that or Prozac.

—LBH

Whoever this woman was, I was taken by her sheer vulnerability. Or maybe it was her honesty. *Is there a difference?* I bookmarked the blog and then got ready for bed, her words stuck in my head. *Is anyone out there? Can you hear me?*

41

Her words were perfect. I wanted to write back, *I know what you mean.* Or maybe just, *I am. Where are you?*

That's what I was thinking when I finally fell asleep.

Chapter
Four

The next day was Saturday and I slept in, waking a little past nine. I woke still thinking about the blog. I got out of bed and went right to my computer and pulled up the site. There was a new post.

Dear Universe,
   Tonight I read an article where a reporter asked a scientist if he believed there was life on other planets. The scientist replied, "The only thing more frightening than the possibility of there being extraterrestrial life out there is the distinct possibility that there's not and we are alone in the universe."
   I suppose that's exactly how I've felt most of my life.

—LBH

Tonight? I had been on the site at 2 a.m. Either she didn't sleep at night or she lived in a different time zone. Somewhere out west. Could it be in my sales region? Oregon? Washington? California?
   As I sat there thinking, a notification popped up on my computer.

Alex,

We have some matches for you!

Below the words were pictures of six women. If I had wondered whether people fudged the truth on the questionnaire, I now had my answer. The women all looked ten to fifteen years older than me. One of them looked like my late aunt.

They had also all described themselves as athletic and fit, but I couldn't imagine any of them running more than a few yards without collapsing. Perhaps their definition of *athletic* was watching golf from their couch.

When I logged in to the dating site I found that all of the women had already messaged me. I wasn't attracted to any of them. In admitting this I felt a twinge of guilt. No one really wants to believe that physical appearances are such a big criteria—but they are. To both men *and* women. It's psychology. One study showed that attractive people got less jail time than unattractive people. These feelings start young. It's why Cinderella is pretty and her stepsisters are ugly, so we'll naturally pull for her. It's also why Prince Charming is always . . . well . . . charming.

I went back and reread my mysterious LBH.

Chapter
Five

The next Monday, the twenty-first, I met up again with Nate and Dale at lunch. We all came in from different places. It was raining, and Nate was soaking wet. He didn't look too happy about it.

"It's raining," I said.

Nate glared at me. "You think?"

Dale said, "Sometimes, when it rains, I find my wife just standing by the window with a sad look on her face." He paused, then added, "It makes me think that maybe I should let her in."

I shook my head. "I have no idea why she stays with you."

"It's my sense of humor. Women love a sense of humor."

"That must be why she married a joke," Nate said.

"That was cruel," Dale said. "But speaking of jokes. Here." He dropped a bumper sticker in front of me. "I bought it in the Newark airport. It reminded me of you."

Dear Algebra,
Stop asking us to find your "X."
She's not coming back.

"Thank you," I said.

"Don't mention it. How goes the hunt?"

"I think people might lie on those dating sites."

Dale laughed. "*Everyone* lies on those sites. A friend of mine met someone online. He talked to her for several weeks before he finally flew out to meet her. When he got there, he didn't recognize her. The woman had chin hair and had put on more than ninety pounds since the photo she'd posted had been taken.

"When he asked her why she'd lied to him, she said, 'Would you have come if you knew what I really looked like?' Which would be like me saying to a client, 'Would you have bought our product if you knew it actually counted clouds instead of cars?' "

"That's reassuring."

"It's human nature," Nate said, "Everyone lies when it comes to describing themselves. Sometimes without even thinking about it."

"Then why did you send me there?"

"You were wallowing, man. You've got to start somewhere."

"Look at this," Dale said, holding up his iPhone. "This confirms my point. This article says that the vast majority of dating site users lie. Men are more likely to lie about their height, and women are more likely to lie about their weight. Both lie about their body type, with almost eighty percent saying they are athletic and fit—a number far exceeding the national average of athletic and fit bodies."

"That would be my experience," I said.

Dale continued. "It says that women are more likely to lie about their age, rounding down to the nearest five, while men lie about their job and income, generously giving themselves huge raises." Dale looked at me. "Did you lie?"

"I said I was a consultant instead of a salesman."

"That's not lying," Dale said. "That's selling."

"What's the difference? I asked.

"You should always round up," Nate said. "Like how did you rate your looks?"

"Eight."

"Snap!" Dale said. "Failure alert."

"See, that's your problem right there," Nate said. "In the real world, outside the Clooney-Pitt matrix, you're a high nine, pushing ten. If you sold our software the way you just tried to sell yourself, you'd be out of a job."

Dale nodded in agreement. "You're underselling, man. *Way* underselling. Those women are rounding up a five to an eight. You're rounding down a ten to an eight. Now there's a five-point gap."

"You're a salesman," Nate said. "You should ace this thing."

"It's not the pitch," I said, "it's the product."

"You know better than anyone that's not true," Dale said. "A good pitch can sell a bad product and a bad pitch won't sell jack."

"You need to rework your pitch," Nate said.

"Pronto. Does the dating site let you revise your profile?"

"I'm not sure it's worth the effort."

"So the first day out fishing you threw some back. No big deal."

"Was there *anyone* of interest?" Dale asked.

"I found someone interesting. Just not on the site. She writes a blog."

"A blogger," Nate said.

"What does she look like?" Dale asked.

"I have no idea."

"What do you mean?"

"Just what I said. There wasn't a picture. Just kind of a silhouette."

"You mean she purposely shadowed her face."

"Yes."

There was a brief pause, then Dale said, "Now, there's a Texas-size red flag. Beautiful people always post their pictures."

"*Vain* people always post their pictures," I said.

Nate said, "Vain or not, I'm with Dale on this one."

"Look, she's beautiful, okay?"

"How do you know?" Nate asked.

"I read her blog."

They both looked at me like I was taking crazy pills. Finally Nate shook his head. "That's admirable, man. Really admirable. I'm just happy for you that looks don't matter. That's going to swing the opportunity door wide open."

"I didn't say that looks don't matter. They're just not *everything*. Jill was beautiful on the outside. This time I want someone I'm attracted to inside and out."

After a moment Nate leaned back in his chair, lacing his fingers behind his neck. "Well, like I said, don't worry about it. It's just the first week. Believe in the process."

"And my blogger?"

"You're a salesman. It's another lead. Doesn't matter where it came from."

Dale glanced down at his watch. "I've got to go. I've got to finish up the paperwork on the Newark sale before the holiday. *Ciao, ragazzi.*"

After he was gone Nate asked, "What are you doing for Thanksgiving?"

"I don't know. Probably watching football with a frozen turkey dinner."

"You're breaking my heart, man. Why don't you spend it with Ashley and me? You know the woman can cook, and I'm deep-frying a turkey. It's going to be epic."

"By *epic* do you mean disaster?"

"Eating a TV turkey dinner alone at Thanksgiving is a *disaster*."

"Is Ashley okay with it?"

"It was her idea. She was feeling sorry for you."

"Now I'm pitiable."

"Yeah, you are." He hit me on the shoulder. "This too shall pass."

"When?"

"I don't know. That's up to God."

"I meant, *when* is dinner?"

He grinned. "Oh. Three. I think. I'll get back to you on that. You ready to go back?"

"I'm going to finish my lunch," I said.

"Yeah, you talk too much," he said, standing. "See you at HQ." He leaned against his cane and limped out into the rain.

That night there were two more dating suggestions. One of them looked a lot like Jill. It took me a minute to realize that it was her. I was tempted to read her self-description but deleted it instead. I guess Clark hadn't worked out. It wasn't seeing her there that bothered me most, it was that she might have seen me there. Why did that feel so humiliating?

I clicked off the site and then over to LBH. I was happy to see that she had posted another blog entry.

Dear Universe,

Last night I came across yet another study about loneliness. You, being a sane person, might ask, "What kind of person does a study on loneliness?" I'll tell you. The same kind of person who spends her nights looking up those studies—a lonely person. And I'm starting to believe that there are more than a few of us.

This study showed that chronic loneliness impacts our bodies as negatively as smoking two packs of cigarettes a day. Not the same way, of course, just the life risk part. And there's more bad news. The article went on to say that lonely people had worse reactions to flu shots than non-lonelies (I think I just made up that word; my computer put a red squiggly line under it) and that loneliness depresses the immune system. In other words, if you're lonely, not even your body wants to be around you, so it tries to off itself.

Maybe that's why I feel like I'm coming down with something tonight. I wish I had someone to rub Vicks menthol on my chest and tuck me into bed. Actually, if I had someone to do that, they'd be in bed with me. Or bringing me hot honey and lemon tea. That would be heaven. But then, if I had someone who loved me like that, I wouldn't be lonely. Then I probably wouldn't be sick.

Sometimes I would still pretend I was.
—LBH

Whoever she was, I was dying to meet her.

Chapter
Six

The next day Dale was out of town so I went out for sushi with just Nate.

"Any more leads?" Nate asked before popping a piece of spider roll into his mouth. I think he was more interested in my dating site experience than I was.

"A few. One of them was Jill."

"They tried to match you up with Jill?"

"Yes, which, for the record, makes me doubt the site's credibility."

"Small world, man. Or maybe it's not a mistake. Maybe Jill's subconsciously still in love with you and she's looking for someone like you."

"Yeah, right," I said, though some twisted part of me wanted to believe it.

"Any other females of interest?"

I shook my head. "Not really. One gal has seven children."

"Wow. I'm surprised that she was forthcoming about it. That's the kind of news you drop after the fourth date. Maybe fifth."

"So, she was being honest. She seemed nice."

"Seven kids? That's not nice you're sensing, it's desperation."

I broke open an edamame. "Yeah, that's a bit too much of a lifestyle change for me."

"What about your blog lady? LOL."

I shook my head. "It's *LBH*. She posted another blog entry."

"Did she leave any clues to her identity?"

"No. Just her initials."

"Good luck with that," he said. "Oh, I told Ashley that you're spending Thanksgiving with us. She was pleased."

"Thanks. I'm looking forward to it."

"And if my turkey doesn't work, at least you won't be alone."

That night I made myself a protein smoothie for dinner, watched an hour of television, and then, as had become my habit, I checked the blog. There was another post. Two, actually.

Dear Universe,

Tonight I was thinking about something my father said to me when I was a girl. My father was German; he had an accent and everything. One day he said to me, when the time comes for you to want a man, wait for the one who brings you edelweiss. I asked him what edelweiss was, and he said, it's a small white mountain flower from the old land. I asked him why, and he said, edelweiss grows very high up in the mountains in rocky terrain. It takes great faith and commitment and courage for a man to pick edelweiss and then bestow it on his love.

I've never forgotten that. I miss my father.

He was such a good man. Where are the men like that? Where is my man with edelweiss?

—LBH

Again her words were beautiful. Was I a man who would bring his love edelweiss? I thought I was. I hoped I was. I read it over again before I started on the next post.

The second entry had been posted an hour before the other.

Dear Universe,

Great (I type sarcastically). I just discovered more science working against me. There was a study that showed that loneliness actually makes people colder. Not just *feel* colder, but actually *be* colder, like making skin temperature drop. It seems like a cruel irony that the coldest people have no one to warm up with.

It's so cold here. Tonight the snow keeps falling, covering everything beneath a silent, cold blanket. The mountains look so pretty painted white. The weatherman says that we might get several feet tonight. The world outside is abandoned. My world inside is abandoned.

I feel so cold tonight. I wish I had someone to hold me.

—LBH

I wish I had someone to hold me. I wished that I was holding LBH. Was I crazy to feel this way about someone I didn't know? I wanted to take her edelweiss.

Then I realized that she'd given me my first clue. *Mountains and snow.* I wondered if I could determine her location using a weather map. I tried. It was snowing in nineteen different states. At least I could mark off all the nonmountainous cities without snow, narrowing my search down to just a hundred million people. No problem.

"Come on, LBH," I said aloud. "Just give me a little more to go on."

Chapter
Seven

Thanksgiving had never been kind to me. You hear stories of families getting together over the holidays only to wreak havoc on each other. That's pretty much my family's story. My memories of Thanksgiving, back when I was home and my grandparents were still alive, consisted of my parents volleying insults back and forth across the table until my mother threw something moist at my father and huffed away. My father would then storm out of the house to the nearest bar, leaving my grandparents and me sitting at the table in silence until my grandmother, who dealt with conflict by pretending it didn't exist, would ask me some benign question like "How's school going?"

I hated the day.

I woke up not feeling well (psychosomatic?), so I slept in. When I couldn't sleep anymore, I watched a little of the Macy's parade and then, on a whim, checked the blog. There was something new.

Dear Universe,
   I know I don't usually post twice a night, but I couldn't sleep. And I found more

science. (You know how I love science.) A neuroscience magazine recently published a theory claiming that loneliness developed as a survival trait. The basic premise is this: to survive as a species, humans had to learn to band together—form communities to help each other thrive. This connection was so important to our survival that our brains developed a biomechanical function that caused us to feel pain (aka loneliness) whenever we found ourselves not connecting with others. Therefore, we experience loneliness the same way we experience other biological needs like tiredness or hunger—as something that drives us to action. So in theory, loneliness is *good* for the species. Good for the whole, bad for the one.

—LBH

I took a deep breath. *That's for sure.* I turned off my computer and got in the shower. I wondered what LBH was doing for Thanksgiving.

I arrived at Nate's house shortly before three. He opened the door before I rang the bell. "Alex, brother. Welcome." We man-hugged. The sound of Mitch Miller's Christmas music filled the home, along with the rich aromas of Thanksgiving baking.

"I hope you came hungry. Ashley has outdone herself."

"I was born hungry. And I'm prepared to abuse my stomach for Ashley's sake."

Nate slapped me on the back, which, incidentally, always hurt. "I like that. Always willing to take one for the team."

"How'd your turkey turn out?"

"Great," he said. "Just took it from the oven."

"I thought you were deep-frying the turkey."

"Yeah, Ashley vetoed that. She read about all these fools burning down their houses on Thanksgiving."

"I vetoed what?" Ashley said, emerging from the kitchen.

"Deep-fried turkey."

"Yeah, can you imagine?" She kissed me on the cheek. "Hi, Alex."

"Hi, gorgeous." Ashley was just about the opposite of Nate. As refined as she was beautiful, she was also petite, barely a hundred pounds. I was afraid that Nate would someday roll over in bed and crush her.

"It smells wonderful," I said to her.

"Thank you. When Nate asked if he could invite you, I changed the menu a little. He told me how much you love pecan pie. So I made you one."

"Will you marry me?"

Ashley shook her head. "No, one man's enough. But I will send you home with the leftover pie."

"At least there's a consolation prize," I said.

Ashley smiled, then said to Nate, "I'm just waiting for the rolls. We'll be eating in about ten minutes. Stay close."

He turned to me. "C'mon, buddy. Let's watch the Dolphins finish off Pittsburgh."

I followed Nate into his den, where the television was tuned to a Dolphins-Steelers game. It was the fourth quarter. The Dolphins led by a touchdown.

"How's your day?" Nate asked.

"It's been all right."

"Any online dating action?"

"You keep asking. You got a bet going on this?"

"Maybe."

"You and Dale bet on whether I'll find someone online?"

"No. We bet on whether or not you'll marry someone you met online."

"I'm speechless."

He was quiet for a moment and then said, "He gave me ten-to-one odds. I'd be a fool to pass that up."

"That's faith."

"For the record, I got a hundred on you that you will. Don't let me down."

Ashley called for us a few minutes later. The three of us gathered around the dining room table, which held far more food than three people could eat. Even when one of them was the size of Nate.

"I'll say grace," Nate said. "We are grateful this day for our great country and our great flag and ask thy blessings upon those who are in harm's way, away from their families today, defending our freedoms. We are grateful for the abundance of our lives and especially, today, for this fine meal. We are grateful for friends, and ask you to bless lonely Alex to find a nice lady to soothe his loneliness. Maybe even his mystery blog lady. Amen."

I looked at him and shook my head. "Thanks."

"Don't mention it," he said. "I've got your back."

Ashley handed me a basket of rolls and asked, "Who's this mystery blog lady?"

"Alex has been stalking a woman on the Internet," Nate said.

"Really?"

"It's not as interesting as Nate makes it sound," I replied.

"It never is," Ashley said. "Which is good, because it sounds really creepy."

"Thanks for making me sound creepy," I said to Nate. "As well as pitiable."

"Those are not mutually exclusive traits."

"So what's the story behind this Internet stalking?" Ashley asked. "That's one thing about Nate's tales: they may be crazy, but there's always some basis in truth. It may be just one percent, but it's always there."

"That's because it's beyond me to conjure something up out of thin air," Nate said. "I simply have no imagination."

"I didn't say that," she said. "So who is this mystery lady, and what does my husband have to do with her?"

"Nate talked me into signing up for an Internet dating service. While I was online, I came across a woman's blog that caught my attention."

"A famous blogger?"

"No. Her site seems pretty small."

"Have you contacted her?"

"I would, except she doesn't post any contact information."

"Which means she doesn't *want* to be contacted." Ashley turned to Nate. "You really sent him to an Internet dating site?"

"Why wouldn't I?"

"You know why not. After what I went through."

"This sounds like a story," I said.

She looked at me, shaking her head. "You don't know the half of it."

Nate shook his head. "You're going to tell him about the eye doctor."

"The *eye* doctor?" I said.

She nodded. "About two months before I met Nate, I met a guy online who was an optometrist. He wasn't especially handsome, but he was a professional and he seemed nice enough. Besides, he was local, so we planned a date.

"At dinner he told me which eyeglass store he worked at; coincidentally, I had been there just a few weeks earlier. I told him that when I was there I had seen some really cute sunglasses I wished I'd bought.

"After dinner he said, 'I'm a manager at the store. If you're serious about those glasses, I can get you anything at cost—less than half price.'

"I really wanted the glasses and I thought that sounded pretty good, so we went to the eye store. I should've realized that something was wrong when we went in through the back door and he told me to be quiet and not look into the security cameras. I asked him why, but he just mumbled something about company protocol, then said, 'Don't worry about it,' which is when I should have started worrying.

"We got in the store and he took me to the showcase with all their glasses, then he stepped into a back room. Neither of us was aware that we'd set off the silent alarm. So after I found the glasses I went to find him, and he's in one of the examining rooms, sitting in a chair, totally naked.

"I'm planning my escape when someone shouts, 'Freeze! Put your hands up.' It's the police, and they're pointing guns at us. I'm totally freaked out, because I think I'm either going to be shot or going to prison, and this nut I'm with is totally naked.

"They took us aside, and after I stopped crying and explained the situation, they had a good laugh and let me go. One of the officers drove me home. My date was a different matter. They told him to put his clothes on, then they hand-cuffed him and took him away. As they were walking him out of the store, he shouted to me, 'Call me.'" She looked at Nate. "That's why you shouldn't have suggested Internet dating."

I grinned. "Yeah, Nate didn't share any of that with me."

"It wasn't relevant," Nate said. "The chances of Alex running into another naked eye doctor are next to nil."

After dinner, Nate and I did the dishes while Ashley spoke on the phone with her mother in Oklahoma. Then all three of us went into the den to eat pie and talk. After a half hour Ashley excused herself to take a nap. Ten minutes later Nate left me to join her. I got another piece of pecan pie and then drove home. Another Thanksgiving bites the dust.

Chapter Eight

The weekend after Thanksgiving was basically a blur. The achiness I had felt Thanksgiving morning wasn't just a passing thing; somehow I had caught a cold, so I spent the next day wiped out, staying mostly in bed or a steaming shower. Jill used to make fun of my "man-colds" as she called them, but she jests at sniffles who never felt a man-cold.

Not that I was missing anything by staying inside—at least nothing that I didn't want to miss. During my early years of marriage, Jill would drag me out of bed while it was still dark for Black Friday shopping. More surprising is that I let her. I hated every minute of it. The event was probably where the differences in our personalities were most keenly revealed. Jill thrived in the crush of holiday shopping chaos, soaking in the sounds, deals, and assault and battery, while I saw the experience more as a consumer's version of Pamplona's running of the bulls, dodging people, trying not to be gored by shopping carts.

After three years of dutifully following her around, I finally admitted to not enjoying the excursion. To my surprise, she admitted to really wanting to shop with her girlfriends instead of me, both of us doing what we didn't want to do because we thought it was what the other wanted—sort of a twisted "Gift of the Magi" thing. From then on, she shopped while I slept. Problem solved.

This year, other than Nate and Dale, I had no one to shop for. As pathetic as it made me feel, and in spite of what Jill had done, I missed her. I wondered if she was out shopping. Of course she was. She had our 401k.

Even though I was sick, I toyed with the idea of going out alone, for tradition's sake, but I couldn't bring myself to do it—not because of my cold so much as my heart. It's an irony that nothing makes you feel more lonely than crowds of people you are not connected to.

I had pretty much written off another wasted holiday until later that night when I went online. That's when LBH wrote something that changed everything.

Dear Universe,
Another Thanksgiving alone. Why do you think it is that we feel our loneliness most keenly during the holidays? I have much to be thankful for. And, in spite of my loneli-ness, I am thankful. I'm healthy. I'm not rich but I have a roof over my head.

I hope all my writing about loneliness doesn't make me seem ungrateful. Sometimes I feel like a whiner. I write not to complain, but for the therapy of it all.

Tomorrow everyone will head out en masse to the stores. Here, many will head to the larger towns. Everywhere there will be crowds, which is why I'll stay in. It's strange to me that I feel most lonely in crowds. Ironic I suppose.

Every September, at a park near my home, this little town holds a Swiss Days festival. As I look out my window at all the people coming and going in their groups, I wonder where they all come from. Humans need to belong. Humans have always needed tribes. Today we find tribes in family or clubs or religion. What happens when we fall out of them? I suppose, in prehistoric times, it was fatal to be cast out of a tribe, to be exiled or excommunicated from the group, away from the people we love and need. Exile from the tribe is a form of execution.

—LBH

Swiss Days? What were Swiss Days? Finally she'd given me something I could go on. I typed "Swiss Days" into Google and three results came up—three different cities: Berne, Indiana;

Midway, Utah; and Santa Clara, Utah. I had never heard of any of these places.

I began searching online for information on the three towns. They were all small, with populations of around four thousand people— about 5 percent the size of Daytona Beach. This was good. The fewer people to sift through the better.

Berne, Indiana, is a town thirty-five miles south of Fort Wayne, settled in 1852 by Mennonite immigrants who came from Switzerland and named their new home after Switzerland's capital city. From the pictures online, it didn't look much like the original Berne.

Santa Clara, Utah, is a southern Utah town near the Arizona border and in the late nineteenth century was largely inhabited by converted Mormon immigrants from Switzerland. It was a desert town and looked mostly flat, though there were distant mountains visible in some images of the city I found.

Of the three towns, Midway looked the most like Switzerland in geography and architecture. It was a lush, hilly area discovered by fur trappers and later settled by Mormon Swiss immigrants. Many of its present-day buildings, including what I assumed was the town hall, were designed after Swiss architectural styles. It was also known for its abundance of natural hot springs.

According to a previous blog entry, the town

LBH lived in had mountains and a lot of snow. While all three locales had mountains or hills, only two received any significant amount of snowfall, Midway and Berne. Berne averaged twenty-seven inches of snow a year, and Midway got more than a hundred. Though Santa Clara was also in Utah, it was nearly three hundred miles south of Midway and averaged less than three inches of snow a year. LBH had written that she was expecting several feet of snow in one night, which disqualified Santa Clara and was improbable for Berne, though it was still a possibility.

Then I looked up the dates of each of the towns' Swiss Days festivals to see which ones were held in September. Berne held their event near the end of July. Santa Clara and Midway held their events in September. Only one of the towns met all the criteria. LBH lived in Midway, Utah.

Wherever the devil that was.

Chapter
Nine

Since my clients were government bureaucrats, the end of the year was always a manic time for sales as city, county, and state officials scrambled to spend their annual budgets lest they find them reduced by their state legislatures the next fiscal year. This trend usually continued at a feverish pace until the end of the second week of December, which was when everything shut down as abruptly as if someone had turned off a faucet. This was why the Traffix management always held our company party on the evening of the second Saturday of December. It's also why nothing got done after that.

Even though our official company break began on December 22, for all intents and purposes, we were closed for business the last half of the month. This was the first year that I wasn't looking forward to all that time off. If Thanksgiving was any indication, it wasn't going to be much of a holiday. Still, it had to be better than the previous December. That's when Jill had left me.

LBH posted blog entries on the Friday, Saturday, and Sunday after Thanksgiving.

78

Dear Universe,

I took a quiz on loneliness last night. I was doing one of my late-night Internet searches and I found a quiz from a psychology magazine titled "How Lonely Are You?" Even though I already knew the answer, I went through the whole quiz, answering things like "How often do you feel that you have no one to talk to?" and "How often do you feel overwhelmed by your loneliness?" I answered OFTEN to every question, except one: "How often do you find yourself waiting for someone to call or write?" That one I responded to with NEVER. There's no one out there who thinks about me enough to call or write. I guess it comes as no surprise that the quiz categorized me as "Extremely Lonely." I didn't need a quiz to tell me that.

—LBH

Dear Universe,

My last few posts have been pretty heavy so I wanted to lighten the mood by posting some jokes about loneliness:

Question: Why didn't the skeleton go to the dance?

Answer: He had no body to go with.

Terrible, I know. Not even worthy of being

on a bubblegum wrapper. How about this one?

There was a man who desperately wanted to be alone, so he built himself a house on top of a mountain. One day there was a knock on the door. When he went to answer it, there was no one there but a snail.

The man, angry that his solitude had been disturbed, picked up the snail and threw it as far as he could.

One year later there was another knock on the door and the man opened it to see the snail again. "What did you do that for?" the snail asked.

For the record, I would have let the snail in.

—LBH

Dear Universe,

There's a famous painting by Edward Hopper called *Nighthawks*. It's a very iconic image. You've probably seen it. The painting is of a downtown diner at night, something I especially relate to. Through the windows you see a man and a woman sitting on one side of the counter, a second man sitting across from them, and a third working behind the bar.

That painting has always struck me as being intensely lonely. Maybe it's because as the viewer you are put in the position of being on the outside, looking in. But even the people on the inside look lonely. When asked about it, Hopper said, "Unconsciously, probably, I was painting the loneliness of a large city."

Unfortunately, large cities don't have a monopoly on loneliness. It can be found in small towns as well. Loneliness can be found everywhere there are people.

That last sentence seems horribly ironic.

—LBH

Monday morning I flew out to Seattle to meet with the city's Traffic Engineering Department, and then, two days later, continued on to Portland to meet with the Oregon Department of Transportation. My meetings went well, though my Seattle clients decided to push back implementation of our product until the new year, something that would shift some of my year-end bonus to next year. I didn't care. I might be lonely, but I was doing well financially, at least.

On my way home from Portland I changed planes in Salt Lake City. I had a window seat and I looked out the window as we prepared to land. Salt Lake City and its surrounding suburbs were white as a bedsheet. It was as if someone had taken a giant can of white spray frost to it. The Rocky Mountains encircling the city were always majestic, but in winter they rose like great heaping banks of snow pushed to the side.

As I sat there looking out over the mountains, I couldn't help but think how close I was to LBH. Midway was just east of the range, about thirty miles. I might have seen the town from the air and not known it. She was down there somewhere. LBH had been silent since Thanksgiving week-end. I wondered why she hadn't been blogging. I realized I was worried about her. Strange that I was worried about someone I didn't know.

I arrived back home Thursday night. Daytona Beach was warm compared to where I'd been the last week, but people still wore coats.

Before going to bed I turned on my computer and pulled up the LBH blog, hoping but not expecting that she'd written something. She had.

Dear Universe,

This is my last entry. If you've been following my ramblings, let me take this moment to say good-bye. I hoped that blogging would help ease my loneliness, but it hasn't. Nothing has. I am so weary of hurting all the time. I think it's time to go home. In my heart, home is not a place. It's a person. It's my father. I miss my father. I miss him every day. I want to see

82

him again. I want to tell him to his face that I am sorry for what I've done.

I plan to stay here until Christmas. For the sake of the season. That's what I'm telling myself. Maybe I'm still hoping that something might change. Hope springs eternal.

I'll leave on New Year's Eve. May you, dear wanderer, find what I couldn't.

—LBH

Her last entry. There was a deep melancholy to her message, deeper than anything she'd posted before. There was a finality to it. My heart ached. I didn't know this woman, yet my heart was breaking for her. I felt loss. I suppose, in a way, I did know her. I knew her because I knew her pain. I knew her because she'd shared her vulnerability and honesty. In that way I'd known her better than someone I'd shared a bed with. I wanted to know her better because of her honesty. And now I knew that if I didn't find her before New Year's, I never would.

Chapter
Ten

The next morning I called Nate. He answered the phone with, "Dude, when'd you get back?"

"Last night. Do you have time for lunch?"

"Yes, sir. I always have time for food."

"Is Dale around?"

"Yes, but he's working from home today. I'll give him a call. What's up?"

"I found her."

"You found who?"

"LBH."

"Your blogger woman," he said. "You spoke with her?"

"I'll tell you about it at lunch."

Two hours later we met up at a steak house not far from the office. Dale was there. As soon as we sat down he said, "So, don't leave us hanging. What's she like?"

"I don't know," I said.

"But you said that you found her," Nate said.

"I know where she lives. In one of her posts she mentioned something called Swiss Days."

Nate's brow furrowed. "She's in Switzerland?"

"No. She's in a small town in Utah called Midway. Every year they have a Swiss Days celebration."

Nate sat back, his expression changing from concern to disappointment. "That can't be the only Swiss Days in the world. There's probably hundreds of them."

"No, there are only three Swiss Days festivals in America, one in Indiana, the other two in Utah. And only one of those matches the date and weather she wrote about."

"Impressive, Sherlock," Dale said.

Nate still didn't look convinced. "So you know the town she lives in. That's a long stretch from knowing who she is. How many people live in this Midway?"

"A little over four thousand people."

"That's not bad," Dale said.

"That's still a lot of people," Nate said.

"Not once you break it down," I said. I took out a piece of paper I'd written some numbers on. "Listen. According to the last census, there were 2,074 females in Midway. Utah has the youngest population in the US, so thirty-six percent are nineteen or under, that leaves one thousand, three hundred twenty-eight possibilities. Finding one of them with the initials LBH can't be that difficult."

"If this sales thing doesn't work out, you could find work as a private investigator," Dale said.

"I just hope she's not catfishing," Nate said.

I looked at him. "What's catfishing?"

"Internet dweebs who pretend they're someone they're not."

"Why would she do that?"

Nate shrugged. "Lots of reasons. Boredom. Thrill of the hunt. Revenge. Insanity."

"He's right," Dale said. "There are stories all over the Internet. There was a British woman who convinced a half dozen women that she was a man named Sebastian. She was courting them all at the same time. One of the women figured it out when her Internet lover posted a picture of 'his' favorite perfume, not realizing that her own image was reflected in the bottle." Dale looked me in the eyes. "In other words, LBH might be a bored, twenty-two-year-old manboy."

"It doesn't make sense," I said. "If she were really trying to 'catfish,' why would she keep her identity hidden?"

"You're right," Nate said. "It would be like running a classified ad in the paper and not leaving a phone number."

"Exactly," I said. "What would be the point?"

"You know," Dale said, "I don't think that finding her will be the most difficult part."

"What do you mean?"

"I mean once you find her, what are you going to say? Excuse me, I found you on the Internet and I tracked you down in Utah. You're going to freak her out. Big-time. If she doesn't deny it's her, she'll probably call the police."

I hadn't thought it through that far. "You're right," I finally said. "I guess I'll jump off that bridge when I reach it."

"So what now?" Nate asked.

I looked at them for a moment, then said, "I guess I'm going to Utah."

Chapter
Eleven

That night was our company party. It was held in downtown Daytona Beach at Bratten's Cove, a swanky seafood restaurant overlooking the ocean. There were a little more than fifty employees there, most with their spouses or partners. I intentionally arrived late. I hated going alone and I didn't want to arrive before Dale or Nate. I did anyway.

I got a glass of merlot, then sat down with a dish of cocktail sauce and a cold plate of peel-and-eat shrimp. I had sat there alone for a half hour when Dale and his wife arrived. Michelle, a stunner, was the best evidence of Dale's sales expertise.

"Hey, how's my favorite wallflower?" Dale said.

"If it isn't Beauty and the Beast," I replied.

"Don't call my wife a beast," Dale said. Michelle just rolled her eyes.

"How does he keep you?" I asked.

"I guess he's a good salesman," she said, hugging me. "How are you, Alex?"

"Hanging in there."

"Dale says you met someone on the Internet?"

"There are no secrets."

"I'm happy for you. She's from Utah?"

"Yes."

"I used to ski in Utah in my college days.

Mostly Deer Valley and Park City. Sometimes Alta. It's really beautiful. You won't believe the mountains out there. They're incredible."

"She lives near Park City," I said.

Michelle's smile grew. "That's really great. You're going to love it. Does 'she' have a name?"

"I'm sure she does," I said. "I just don't know it."

Michelle looked at me and then at Dale with an amused grin. "I can't tell if he's kidding."

Dale shook his head. "He's not. It's complicated."

Michelle hesitated for a moment, as if still trying to figure things out, then said, "Well, I hope things work out."

"Thank you. Me too."

Dale saluted. "We're going to get something to eat. When are you leaving?"

"Tomorrow."

"Good luck, buddy. Keep in touch."

"Will do."

They wandered off to the food table with all the other couples.

The evening just got more depressing. Technically, the party was great. The food was great. Everyone looked great. Everyone seemed to be having a good time. I just kept drinking and peeling shrimp. I was finally about to leave when Nate walked up to me.

"Dale said I'd find you here."

I looked up at him. "Where have you been?"

He groaned as he sat down next to me. "Just as we were walking out of the house, Ashley's sister called. She got in a big fight with her husband and was crying buckets. Ashley was on the phone with her for an hour. I finally had to drag her out to the car."

"Where is she?"

"She's still in the car talking to her."

"I'm sorry."

"Hold on, I'm going to get a drink." He returned a minute later holding a short glass. "So, I'm glad we're alone. I wanted to talk to you."

"About what?"

"I'm worried. Are you really going to Utah to find that woman?"

"Yes."

He frowned. "Is now really the best time?"

"It's the perfect time. I don't have any appointments until January."

"I mean . . . emotionally. You know how it is, the holidays can make you kind of . . ."

"What? Crazy?"

"Yes," he said, owning up to his concern. "Being alone during the holidays can make you crazy. I looked up LBH on the Internet. It's code for *Let's be honest*. Think about it. Isn't that what you liked about the blog entries—her honesty? What if those aren't even her real initials?"

I had considered the possibility but had always pushed it from my mind. "Then I'm screwed."

"Exactly. So why not wait?"

I took another drink, then said, "Because she posted her last entry. She wrote that she's going home, wherever that is, and she's leaving on New Year's Eve. If I don't find her before New Year's, I'll never find her."

Nate continued to look at me grimly.

"I take it you don't approve."

"No, I don't. You don't know her name, you don't know anything about this woman."

"I know." I took a breath. "Look, it's hard to explain, but it's like there's this voice inside telling me that I've got to do this. Maybe it's desperation. Maybe it's just crazy, but it's there. I feel it."

"You're right," Nate said. "It *is* crazy. It's a lunatic affair."

"So what if it is? Look at me. I'm all alone drinking while everyone else is having a good time. I've been doing *predictable* and *sane* for my whole life, and where has it gotten me? I'm thirty-two, divorced, lonely, living in an apartment I hate, working the same job for the last decade, and watching Netflix alone every night before going to bed. Maybe it's time I tried something crazy."

Nate didn't answer.

"Haven't you ever just had a feeling deep in

95

your heart that you needed to do something, even if you didn't know why? Even if it seemed a little *crazy?*"

He was quiet for a moment, then said, "Yes. I have."

"So do I ignore it? Do I pretend it's not there?"

Again he didn't answer.

"Have you forgotten what it was like before Ashley?"

Nate shook his head. "No. I remember." His mouth rose in a sad smile, then he reached over and patted me on the shoulder. "Do what you need to do, brother. Good luck."

"Thanks."

"When do you fly out?"

"Tomorrow around noon."

"Where do you land?"

"Salt Lake City. I've got a rental car. Midway's only an hour's drive from the airport."

"Are there any decent hotels?"

"I'm staying at a little place called the Blue Boar Inn. If it's half as nice as it sounds on the Internet, I will be very happy."

He smiled. "I hope the same is true of LBH."

Chapter
Twelve

My flight landed at Salt Lake City International Airport around half past four. Even though I'd been through it just days before, it seemed different. It was the first time I'd landed there as a final destination.

The airport was decorated for the holidays with tinsel snowflakes pinned to the walls and hanging from the tile ceiling by wire.

As I stepped outside the terminal the cold hit me like a slap. It rarely gets below seventy degrees in Daytona Beach, so I didn't have much (actually any) experience with nostril-freezing cold—which is exactly what the cold did. It froze the inside of my nose as it turned each breath into a visible cloud.

I had brought the warmest coat I owned, a sheepskin-lined leather aviator jacket, but against this kind of a cold it was about as much protection as Bubble Wrap on a demolition derby car. Just dragging my bag across the terminal road to the car rental center was enough to convince me that I would probably be investing in a parka. How did people live in such cold weather? *Why* would they?

Truthfully, I felt a little wimpy as I looked over and saw, on the curb near the passenger pickup, two teenagers wearing nothing but shorts and T-shirts. For the record, one of them was shaking and both were hugging themselves, so at least they were not oblivious to the cold. I guess coats aren't cool but hypothermia is.

The man at the car rental booth asked if I was going to one of the ski resorts.

"No. Midway."

"Same thing," he said. "You're just next to Park City. You should have four-wheel drive for the snow."

"Is there a lot of snow?"

He smiled. "Yeah."

He upgraded me to a Ford Explorer and within ten minutes I was on my way to Midway.

Following my GPS, I drove the I-215 freeway south to I-80 east toward the mountains until I reached the mouth of the canyon. The guy at the car rental wasn't kidding about snow. Snow-covered rock walls rose more than a hundred feet above me on both sides of the freeway. It was beautiful but made me feel anxious and claustrophobic. The traffic was somewhat heavy, not just because of the weather conditions, but because it was six o'clock and I had hit the tail end of rush hour.

I passed the sign for the Park City and Deer Valley ski resorts, then took exit 146 for US-40 toward Heber/Vernal. No mention of Midway. Fortunately, the man at the rental car place had also told me that Heber and Midway were sister cities and even many of the locals didn't know where one ended and the other began. About ten miles after the exit, a sign directed me west toward Midway and I turned off the highway.

Midway was more rural than I had imagined, and both sides of the two-lane road were lined with snow-covered trees, pastures, and red, rustic, snowcapped barns. It looked like something out of a Grandma Moses painting.

I crossed a bridge over a small river and followed the road west past a roundabout with a miniature bell tower in the center, then farther west past a development of Swiss-style chalets, until the road ended in a *T*. On the side of the road there was a round wooden post with blue metal signs that pointed south to several resorts and one that pointed north, with the words *The Blue Boar Inn*.

I turned right. The narrow road wound between more open fields for a hundred yards until it curved west again leading up to a large Swiss chalet. On the wall of a second-story balcony, overhanging the flags of America, Switzerland, France, and Germany, was the inn's logo—a blue, tusked boar painted above a flourish of olive leaves. In Gothic lettering it read:

THE BLUE BOAR INN

On the front corner of the property was a large bronze statue of a boar. Both sides of the road were lined in thick, ice-crusted snowbanks nearly four feet tall.

The inn's cobblestone driveway had been cleared and I drove up to the front door beneath a brook stone façade overhang with a massive Alpine clock. I got my bag out of the backseat and walked up the stairs.

There was a large Christmas wreath on the arched front door, encircling a door knocker, a boar's head made of dark, rustic metal.

I pulled open the door and walked inside, stepping onto the parquet floor of an elaborately decorated lobby. The room smelled of cinnamon and apple, and a dozen or so poinsettias lined the tile floor.

The dining room was directly ahead of me, a luxurious, red velvet curtain pulled back to one side of the room as if revealing the opening of a show. On the far side was a large, intricately decorated Christmas tree.

The inn was every bit as luxurious as the webpage had described it to be. More so. I thought of Nate's words, hoping that I would be as impressed with LBH as I was with the inn.

I was admiring a picture of a boar set in a frame made of deer antlers, when someone said, "That etching is from the seventeen hundreds."

I turned back to see a petite Asian woman

standing at the counter, smiling at me. "Are you Mr. Bartlett?"

"Yes. How did you know?"

"You're the last of our guests to check in. Welcome to the Blue Boar Inn."

"Thank you," I said, walking up to the reception counter. "This place is beautiful."

"Thank *you* for appreciating the work we've put into it. The owners have gone to extraordinary lengths to make this inn special. I'm afraid much of it is missed." She glanced down at her computer screen and said, "We have you registered for the William Shakespeare Room."

"That's right."

"I have you down for nine days, departing the following Tuesday morning, the twenty-second, is that correct?"

"Yes, ma'am. If I need to extend my stay a little longer, would that be a possibility?"

"You think you might be staying longer?"

"I'm not sure, but it's possible. I don't know exactly how long I'll be in town. I'm a little bit in limbo."

She looked back down at her computer screen. "As of right now your room is open until Christmas, but if we start to fill up I'll let you know." She set a guest form on the ledge between us. "If you'll just sign here."

She handed me a pen and I signed the form.

"Your room is on the second floor. I'll lead you

up." She retrieved a key from a wall cubbyhole and walked out of the back room, joining me in the lobby.

Bag in hand, I followed her up a circular staircase. The lower half of the staircase walls and banister were stained and polished, dark wood beneath an oxblood-red plastered wall. The lighting fixtures on the wall were electric candle-shaped bulbs mounted to small deer antlers.

The second-floor landing had a hallway on one side with the other open to the dining room below. My room was at the top of the stairway across from the inn's library.

The antique wooden door had an inset hand-carved wood panel of a hare, hung by its feet. Above the door was painted, in delicate calligraphy:

William Shakespeare

"The Shakespeare is one of my favorite rooms," she said as I read the words above the door. She unlocked the door with the heavy key and pushed it open. "After you."

I stepped into the room. It was large with a tiled, European fireplace in the center. The south wall was mostly paned windows, and in the center of the room was a large, four-poster bed. The floor was covered by a black wool carpet.

"Do you like to read, Mr. Bartlett?"

"Yes."

"Just across the hall is our library. And right here, in keeping with the room's name, is our collection of Shakespeare. All of our rooms are named for authors—Shakespeare, Austen, Dickens, Thoreau, Brontë, Chaucer—the classical writers." She smiled at me. "If all is well, I'll leave you to your room. Breakfast is served between six and ten. We are well known for our breakfasts, which are complimentary for our guests. And there's always something to snack on in the dining room. Right now, there's some lemon-blueberry bread you may help yourself to."

"Is there somewhere close you would recommend for dinner?"

"Our own restaurant, of course. We're very proud of it." She smiled again. "You won't need to make reservations, just come on down. It's open tonight until ten."

"Thank you," I said.

"I hope you have a good stay, Mr. Bartlett. My name is Lita. If there's anything I, or my staff, can do to make your visit more pleasant, just let us know."

She handed me my room key. It had a large circular pewter key chain with the inn's embossed crest. "The door doesn't lock by itself so you'll need to use the key. If you leave the inn, feel free to leave your key at the front desk. That way, you won't have to lug it around and we'll know when your room is vacant for service."

"Thank you."

"Thank you for staying with us." She stopped at the doorway. "If you don't mind me asking, what brings you to Midway?"

"I'm looking for someone."

She looked at me with a quizzical expression. "Well, they shouldn't be too hard to find. Midway's not that big a town. Good night."

"Good night," I said.

After she left, I locked the door and looked around the room. The bed was king-size and at least three feet off the ground, resting on a dark oak wooden frame. On the adjacent wall was a tall crested armoire of cherry and birch veneer, elaborately carved in Old English designs.

I opened the armoire's bottom drawer and emptied the whole of my suitcase into it, with the exception of my shirts, which I hung in the upper section.

I slipped off my shoes, then climbed up onto the bed. Without pulling down the covers, I lay back on the padded duvet cover. The concierge's parting words came back to me. *They shouldn't be too hard to find.*

I hoped she was right.

Chapter
Thirteen

About an hour later my hunger exceeded my tiredness, so I washed up and headed back downstairs.

The dining room wasn't crowded. There were only three tables of couples, but it sounded like more, as they were all talking and laughing, happy to be in each other's company. Pachelbel's *Canon in D* played lightly from the room's sound system.

I was again greeted by Lita. "Hello, Mr. Bartlett. Would you like to join us for dinner?"

"Yes, thank you."

"Follow me, please." She seated me at a small table for two near the front of the restaurant, away from the other guests. "Is this acceptable?"

"Perfectly."

She smiled at me, then handed me a sheet of white paper and a heavy leather menu. "Someone will be right out to take your order."

As she walked away, I looked down at the paper she'd given me. It contained information on the room's antiques.

The dining area consisted of two rooms, and the walls were painted a distinct green, a shade between fern and dark olive drab. The interior room was a darker hue than the outer and both were abundantly decorated with paintings and antiques.

On the north wall was a carved wooden crest of the Habsburg dynasty. Crossbows were mounted on either side of it. According to my paper, they had all seen battle.

The rooms were lit by three chandeliers made of varying sizes and types of antlers. I was in a world very different from the Spanish-infused setting of Florida.

A young, wholesome-looking woman with short blond hair brought me a cloth-covered bread basket. "Our bread is baked on the premises," she said, folding back the fabric to reveal two kinds of bread. She was obviously a young local and was earnestly trying to appear as sophisticated as possible. "Sourdough and wheat. May I get you something to drink?"

"Do you have a wine list?"

"Yes, sir. I'll bring it right out."

She returned with the list and I looked through their selection, then back over my menu. I ordered the chicken scaloppine with a glass of chardonnay. Then I returned to my inspection of the room, trying not to look as alone as I was, which reminded me of what LBH had written about how embarrassed we are to appear lonely.

Just fifteen minutes later my waitress brought out my soup, a butternut squash bisque. This was followed by the chicken scaloppine with baked spaetzle and asparagus spears. For dessert I had cheesecake. Everything was delicious.

When my waitress brought me my bill, she asked, "Are you staying in the inn?"

"Yes."

"Which room shall I bill this to?"

"The Shakespeare."

My response seemed to please her. "I love that room. But they're all nice. If you get a chance, you should have someone show you around. Our pub in back is especially amazing."

"I didn't know there was a pub."

"It's called Truffle Hollow," she said. "It's small, but pretty cool."

I charged the bill to my room and decided to take a walk around the inn. I followed a hallway back to the pub. Mounted along the wall were two large display cases with hundreds of collector pins from the 2002 Winter Olympics. I paused to look at them, but there were too many to devote much attention to them.

As I made my way back to the lobby, passing through the hall near the kitchen, I came to two paintings. Both were set in either kitchens or restaurants, which was appropriate for their location, and the first, to me, was especially haunting—a portrait of a waitress in an apron standing before a table. It was titled *Ester*. There was something about the look in the woman's eyes that I was drawn to. Something honest. Strong, yet vulnerable.

According to a gold plate on the wall, the artist's name was Pino. I didn't know anything about him and I vowed to look him up.

It felt late, especially since I was still on Eastern Standard Time, so I went up to my room and got ready for bed. I wondered what tomorrow would bring.

Chapter
Fourteen

When I woke the next morning, the window blinds were glowing. I rolled over onto my back, feeling the soft mattress contour with my body. Maybe it was the elevation or the fresh air, but I hadn't slept that well in a long time.

I climbed out of bed and lifted one of the blinds. It was bright and blue outside, subfreezing, and droplets of water had condensed inside my window. *Beautiful,* I thought. *Just beautiful.* I was glad that LBH lived in such a beautiful setting. It seemed fitting.

I showered and dressed, then went downstairs to the dining room. There was music playing, though it was contemporary, not the holiday music that had played the evening before.

There were about four other groups dining, and I seated myself at a table set for two. A waiter soon came out holding a wooden menu, the cover engraved with the inn's trademark boar.

I ordered the buttermilk griddle cakes with fruit, and less than ten minutes later the waiter returned with my meal. I had just started to eat when four elderly women and one man walked into the dining room. The man, who was gray-haired and large of tooth and nose, glanced at me, then left the women and walked up to my table.

"Are you alone, sir?" he asked.

"Yes."

He smiled broadly. "My name is Herr Niederhauser. But you may call me Ray. I am the innkeeper." He stated this with only slightly subdued pride.

"It's a pleasure to meet you. Are you German?"

"Only in spirit. But I speak Deutsch. In my youth I lived in Germany for a few years. Would you mind if I joined you?"

"Not at all. Please."

He pulled out the chair across from me and sat. Then he raised his finger at the waiter, who made a beeline to our table. "Yes, Ray."

"Gary, may I please have a coffee with ham and eggs? And I'll need utensils."

"Of course."

The waiter hurried to the kitchen.

"How is your meal?" Ray asked.

"I just started eating. But good so far."

"If you're here for Sunday brunch, you must try the Scotch eggs. Nothing like them in the world. Are you staying at the inn?"

"Yes, sir."

"What room?"

"The Shakespeare Room."

"Ah. Lovely room. One of my favorites. And how are your accommodations?"

"Everything is wonderful," I said.

"Very good, very good. Wonderful is our goal.

We do our best to pay special attention to detail."

"So you're the innkeeper," I said.

"Yes, sir."

"How long have you been with the inn?"

"Almost eighteen years now, ever since the Warnocks purchased the property. Mrs. Warnock is my wife's cousin. We were dining with them in Park City when Mr. Warnock mentioned this property he had seen in the local real estate papers. We finished our dinners and drove to Midway that very evening. If my memory serves me, the Warnocks purchased the inn the next day.

"Of course, it didn't look like this back then. It used to be called the Huckleberry Inn. Mr. Warnock didn't want to tell his hunting buddies that he owned an inn called the Huckleberry, so he changed the name to the Blue Boar after an old pub in Oxford, England—which not coincidentally was mentioned in the legends and ballads of Robin Hood. There's a framed picture of a woodcut in your room showing Robin Hood and the Tinker sitting in front of the Blue Boar Inn."

"I saw that," I said.

"Our boar logo," he said, motioning to it on my key chain, "came from a three-hundred-year-old woodcut Mr. Warnock found in his travels."

"So the inn's English, not Swiss?"

"It's European. I would call the inn's design more Alpine than Swiss," he said. "The Warnocks remodeled the inn and we've been busy ever since. Of course, things really took off after Utah hosted the Winter Olympics in 2002. The Olympics were a special time." Again, a large smile crossed his face. "Among our guests we had the IOC members from Russia and Norway. The Russians didn't speak English, but they spoke *Deutsch*, as do I, so we communicated quite well."

"How did they find the inn?" I asked.

"I found them. I went over to Soldier Hollow, where they were building part of the Olympic venue, and invited them over for breakfast. It's easy to become friends over good food."

He suddenly laughed. "Ah, but when they came back over for the games, things really got interesting. The Russians arrived with a truckful of luggage—more than two dozen cases. They dropped them off by the front door and said, 'We'll be back to figure out what to do with them.' A half hour later a truck from the Utah National Guard arrived. The driver said he had a delivery for the Russian IOC delegation. Then the soldiers pulled back the tarp covering the truck and there were twenty-two cases of vodka. 'Where would you like them?' he asked."

Ray laughed jovially and slapped the table. "What a time, what a time. If you get a chance, you'll have to look at my Olympic pin collection. It's in the hallway on the way to Truffle

Hollow. I have one thousand, one hundred and eighty pins."

"I saw it last night," I said. "It's impressive."

"I would hope so. It cost me a few groceries to collect them all."

"What did you do before you came to manage the inn?"

"I was a peddler," he said. "I sold high-end skiwear. And what about you?"

"I'm a peddler too. I sell technology."

"Ah. I was never so smart."

"I don't believe you," I said.

"It takes more heart than brains to be an innkeeper. It's the Golden Rule. Give them the hospitality that you would like for yourself."

"That sounds pretty intelligent to me."

The waiter returned with Ray's ham and eggs. Ray cut into the ham steak, took a bite, then asked, "Where are you from?"

"Daytona Beach, Florida."

"Racing capital of the world."

"Have you been there? Or are you a racing fan?"

"Neither. I once had someone stay here from Daytona Beach. I have a good memory that way. I looked the city up on the Internet. It's beautiful."

After I'd finished eating, Ray said, "If you have a minute, I'll show you around."

"I'd like that," I said.

We both stood, and he led me over to the west

wall of the interior dining room. "These paintings once hung in a very famous Paris restaurant. They were painted in 1852 by Jean-Maxime Claude. The building went through the war, and the only reason these paintings weren't looted was because they were set into the walls." He stepped closer. "Now, notice the cabbage in this painting. Originally, this dining room was painted brown, but Mrs. Warnock didn't like the brown walls, so she matched the two greens in this cabbage and painted the dining room after them." He grinned. "I told you, there is much special attention here."

He led me down the hallway, past his Olympic pin collection, to the Truffle Hollow pub.

"The truffle is the boar's mainstay, so it was natural that we named the pub after it," Ray said as we walked inside. "This wooden sign outside the door is a replica of one the Warnocks found in England. Come sit."

There were about a dozen identical tables in all, and I sat down at one in the center of the room. Ray picked up a few nuts from a small dish of pistachios on the table and began to crack them open.

"Let me tell you about this room. The bar here was originally a travel trunk from the 1600s. You can see the locks on it."

The case was about four feet high and twice that long.

"How would someone carry a case that large?" I asked.

"Servants, no doubt. But she's beautiful, isn't she? The floor in here is made of southern pine imported from a World War I airplane hangar in North Carolina. And these tables all came from a bar in Austria. They've been together for more than one hundred and fifty years. But this table is especially valuable. Look here." He tapped the outer edge of the table. There was a brass plaque that read *Ray's Place.*

"Not bad," I said.

"I will live in infamy." He pointed up to the lamp above the bar. One half of it was a wooden carving of a woman's upper body, the other half were deer antlers. "This lamp is from the sixteenth century. The style is called *Lusterweibchen.*" He grinned. "It means 'lustful wench.' There's one just like it upstairs in the library."

"I saw it," I said.

"Then you've seen the library. Beautiful, is it not?"

"Every room I've seen in the inn is beautiful," I replied.

He stood. "Well, I'd better get back to work."

"Thanks for the tour," I said.

"You're very welcome."

As we headed back to the lobby, we walked down the hall with the two paintings I'd admired the night before. "I love these paintings," I said.

He stopped in front of them. "Both of these are by Pino. Are you familiar with Pino?"

"I had never heard of him until yesterday. But I was planning to look him up."

"Interesting man. Pino Daeni was an Italian artist who came to America and did book covers. He was one of the highest-paid cover illustrators in the world. He did many of Danielle Steel's book covers.

"Near the end of his career he grew weary of the publishers' deadlines and turned his attention to fine art, such as these. These two paintings are from his kitchen collections."

"Are they prints?" I asked.

He hesitated for just a moment, then said, "Between us, never to be shared, no. They are originals. We do not want people to know this because of their value." He turned back to the wall. "There is an especially interesting story behind these two paintings. Many years ago, a friend of the inn's owner had purchased a box of assorted wallpaper at a garage sale. She had them in her basement for nearly ten years when her daughter began rummaging through them. When she unraveled one of the rolls of wallpaper she found these two paintings rolled up inside of them."

"You hear stories like that," I said. "It's never happened to me."

"Don't give up yet. There is a lot of hidden treasure in this world," he replied. "Much of it human."

I nodded. "I agree with you. In a way, that's what brought me here."

"What do you mean?"

"I'm looking for someone."

"Someone?"

"A woman."

"Aren't we all," he said. "Let me tell you, you could do worse than Midway. There aren't many available women, but the ones I know are the salt of the earth."

"I'm looking for a specific woman."

He looked at me with intrigue. "Oh? Perhaps I could help you in your quest. What is her name?"

"That's the problem. I don't know her name."

He grinned. "That will definitely complicate things."

"All I know are her initials. LBH."

He rubbed his chin. "Very interesting. And how did you come to know this LBH?"

"I would say that I met her on the Internet, except we haven't really met. She writes a blog, and I just kind of fell for her." I thought he might think me crazy, but instead he looked at me as if with newfound admiration.

"My friend, I already thought you were an interesting fellow, but I was low in my estimation. You are a true romantic. I will do anything I can to help you find this woman. Where will you begin?"

"She wrote that she lived close to where the Swiss Days festival is held."

"That's the community center, the large Alpine building on Main Street. There's a park behind it."

"I was hoping to find some kind of registry of residents' names. Does Midway have a city hall?"

"Yes, the city offices are near the community center. I'll write the address down for you. Neither is far from here." He smiled. "It's a small town, nothing in Midway is far from here." He retrieved a colorful tourist map of Midway and penciled out the route to the city offices. As he handed it to me he said, "Just tell them Herr Niederhauser
sent you."

"Thank you."

"My pleasure. May you find your woman."

Chapter
Fifteen

Our tour had taken more than an hour. It was nearly noon when I walked out of the inn. The cold air was exhilarating. My breath clouded in front of me, billowing like a tailpipe.

As I walked to my car I was again astounded by the beauty and serenity of my snow-covered surroundings. Across the street from the inn was a golf course, covered with a large, crystalline blanket, sparkling with the high sun.

I got into my car, the cold vinyl stiff against my weight. I turned the heater on high, then looked down at my map. The route to the Midway city offices seemed simple enough.

Initially I mistakenly pulled up to the Midway community center. The building looked like a city hall. It was large and had the traditional Swiss-Alpine decoration with gingerbread eaves and a large clock. The door was locked and it was dark inside. It must have been noon because, as I walked back to my car, the clock began to ring. Then Swiss music with yodelers began playing. I looked up to see wooden figurines in Swiss lederhosen dancing around, like a massive cuckoo clock. I watched until the clock completed its show, then got back into my car and, consulting Ray's map again, drove to the city offices.

● ● ●

The city office building looked a little like a church, with a gabled roof and a large clock tower in the middle of the structure. A man was walking down the sidewalk in front of the building with what looked like a fertilizer or seed spreader. He was twisting the handle and something was flying out.

I parked my car and got out. "Getting an early start on fertilizing the lawn?"

He looked at me like I was an idiot. "It's rock salt. I'm salting. So you don't slip and fall and sue the city."

"You're onto me," I said.

He just walked on.

The sidewalk forked when it reached the building. On a sign in the middle of the fork was an arrow pointing left, to *City Recorder*, the other pointed right, to *Mayor*.

I walked to the recorder's office. Hanging on the doorknob was a sign, *Will Return At* . . . with a little clock dial turned to four o'clock.

I retraced my steps to the other side of the building. I stomped the snow off my feet on the mat outside. As I opened the door I was greeted by a rush of warm air. At a desk near the middle of the room a fortysomething woman with bright red hair glanced up at me from a Mary Higgins Clark novel.

"Good afternoon," she said, looking a little

annoyed that I had disturbed her reading. "May I help you?"

"Yes, I need some help locating someone. I was wondering if you could help me."

She set down her book. "Locating who?"

I suddenly felt the awkwardness of my task. "She's someone who lives in Midway. She's a blogger."

The woman just looked at me. "Does she have a name?"

"Her initials are LBH."

"You don't know this person's name?"

"No. I was hoping you'd have some kind of a list of residents."

"No," she said flatly.

"Is there someone else who could help me? Is your boss here?"

Her eyes narrowed. "I'm the *mayor*."

"I'm sorry."

Having worked with city officials for the last decade, I deduced that I had just killed any chance for governmental assistance. To my surprise she said, "Perhaps you should talk to our city treasurer and recorder."

"Thank you. How would I reach them?"

"*Them* are the same person. Just a moment." She rooted around her desk for a moment, then walked over to me holding a business card. "Brad isn't in right now. You should be able to find him at home."

I took the card. "It's okay to go to his home?"

"Yes," she said, as if she were talking to a three-year-old. "That's why I gave you his home address."

"Right. Thank you."

"Please shut the door on the way out. It's cold."

I'm sure that I was as glad to leave the mayor's office as she was to see the back of me. I got in my car and input the address into my phone's GPS system. To my dismay, it couldn't find the address. After a few more minutes of trying, I walked back into the mayor's office.

"Back so soon," she said snarkily.

"Sorry. Could you help me find this address? My phone's GPS can't find it."

"Come here."

I walked over to her desk and she took out a piece of paper and started drawing lines on it. "This is Main Street. We are here. Go down a quarter mile to Holstein Way and turn left. Brad's the third or fourth house on the left. It's a two-story chalet-looking thing, but everything here's a chalet-looking thing, so just look for the gargantuan RV, one of those Death Star–size Winnebagos." She handed me the paper. "You can't miss it. Unless you don't know what a Winnebago is."

"Thank you."

"What's your name, anyway?"

"Alex Bartlett."

"Like the pear?"

"Yes."

"Where are you from, Mr. Bartlett?"

"Daytona Beach, Florida."

She lifted her phone and took a picture of me.

"You wanted my picture?" I said.

"You came all this way to find someone you don't know. I can only hope your motives are not homicidal. If they are, I now have your picture. That should, at least, give you pause."

For a moment I just looked at her. "I wasn't planning on killing anyone while I'm in town. Have a nice day."

It wasn't hard to find the recorder-treasurer's house. The home was, as the mayor had informed me, constructed in the Alpine style, with the characteristic wood shutters with tulips cut into them. On the front of the house there was both an American and a Swiss flag. And there was the Winnebago. I could see why the mayor had used the RV as a landmark—the thing was massive.

I parked my car in his driveway because the snowbank in front of the house was nearly as tall as my car and protruded well out into the street.

After I rang the doorbell, it took a few minutes before someone answered, a woman in her midforties, wearing a sweat suit, leg warmers, and a headband, like a 1980s aerobics throwback. Or a Richard Simmons impersonator. She was red-faced and slightly huffing and I assumed that I had just interrupted her Jane Fonda workout.

"May I help you?" she asked.

"I'm looking for Brad Wilcox."

"Brad's in the shower."

She just stood there. I wasn't sure what I was supposed to do with that. I finally said, "I'll come back."

"What is the nature of your visit? Is this governmental?"

"You could say that."

"Come inside. He's not one to leave a constituent out in the cold."

"Thank you."

I stepped inside the house and she quickly shut the door behind me. "Wipe your feet or take your shoes off."

"I'll take them off," I said, slipping the loafers from my feet.

"You can sit on the sofa there. Would you like a hot cider?"

"Thank you, no."

"All right. He shouldn't be more than an hour."

An hour?

She walked downstairs and a moment later I heard music start up. Eighties music: Wham!, Dire Straits, Supertramp, Duran Duran, Tears for Fears, a-ha.

After about half an hour the music stopped. Still, no one came up or out.

About ten minutes after the music stopped, a man, bald and wearing a robe, walked out into the kitchen. He opened the fridge, took out a glass bottle of milk (when was the last time I'd seen a glass bottle of milk?), drank from it, then turned around. He was startled to see me.

"Who are you?"

I stood. "My name is Alex Bartlett."

"Bartlett. Like the pear?"

"Yes."

"You related to the Bartletts in Lehi?"

"Where?"

"Lehi. Traverse Mountain area."

"Uh, no. I'm not from here. Are you Brad Wilcox?"

"You should know that. You're in my home."

"Your wife told me to wait here for you."

"My sister," he said. "I'm not married." He put the milk back into the fridge, then came to the edge of the room where I was sitting and asked, "What can I do for you?"

"I'm looking for someone."

"Are you a private investigator or a bounty hunter?"

"Neither. It's personal."

"Who are you looking for?"

"I don't know her name. Just her initials."

Just then his sister walked up the stairs and into the kitchen. She had large patches of sweat under her arms.

"You forgot to get more milk," Brad said to her.

"Chill, man. I haven't been to the store yet. I had to exercise. And this guy came to the door."

He turned back to me. "You're looking for someone but you don't know their name?"

"No, sir."

"What is the nature of your manhunt?"

"I've been following her blog."

"Her what?"

"He said *blog*," his sister said. "It's when people write on the Internet."

"Why can't you get her name from the Internet?"

"She only put her initials."

"What initials?"

"LBH."

He squeezed his chin. "Lima Bravo Hotel. Doesn't ring any bells. Did said female write something offensive?"

"No, sir. Actually, the opposite."

"You're a fan of this Internet blog?"

"You might say so."

"Then you're one of those stalkers."

"No."

"You're not stalking her?"

"No, I'm just . . . I want to meet her."

They both just looked at me. Then Brad said, "It would not be prudent for me to be a party to any such affair. We do not have records available to the public."

"You don't have any records?"

"I didn't say that. I said we don't have records *available to the public.* I have billing records for utilities and water but I am not at liberty to share that data with John Q. Public, i.e., you. So, unless there's something else I can help you with, I'll see you to the door."

"No," I said. "That would be it. Thank you."

I walked back to the door, slipped my shoes back on, and then walked out to my car. *These Midway people are interesting.*

On Main Street I found a grocery store, where I bought some bottled water and a premade turkey salad. I ate in my car, then drove back to the inn. I lay down on my bed fully intending to think about my next step, but fell asleep instead. I woke around eight and went downstairs for dinner. There were only two other tables occupied in the dining room.

Lita walked up to me holding a menu. "Would you like dinner, Mr. Bartlett?"

"Yes. Thank you."

She led me to a quiet section of the dining room and handed me the menu. "Have a nice dinner."

A moment later a waiter came out. "What will it be tonight?"

"I'd like the escargots to begin."

"Very good. And for your main course?"

"I'll have the salmon."

"Seared salmon with artichoke and squash. What will you have to drink?"

"A glass of your pinot noir, please."

"A very good choice." He took my menu and walked away.

There was a local newspaper on a side chair and I picked it up. On the front page was a picture of the mayor talking about the importance of tourism and attracting Park City visitors. All I could think of was how she thought I'd come to kill someone.

My escargots came five minutes later along with my wine.

I had just started to eat when someone said, "Snails; nothing like snails with a fine glass of burgundy." I looked up to see Ray walking into the dining room.

"You're working late," I said.

"Not working, Mr. Bartlett. I came back for my glasses and stopped in Truffle Hollow for a drink. May I join you?"

"Please. Would you like some escargots?"

"I love escargots, but not after Scotch." He pulled the chair out across from me and looked at my glass. "What are you drinking?"

"Pinot noir."

"A complicated grape. What did you order for dinner?"

"The salmon."

"You chose well," he said, lightly nodding. "So how was your day, Mr. Bartlett? *Fruitful?*"

I think he meant the comment as some kind of pun on my name. "No. The city wasn't much help."

"You went to the city offices?"

"Yes. I followed your map."

"And they weren't helpful? Surprising." His bushy eyebrows fell. "You didn't run into Jan, did you?"

"Is she the mayor?"

"Jan's the mayor."

"Yes, I met her."

He grimaced. "I'm sorry."

"She wasn't much help."

"No. I don't imagine she would be. I hope you didn't use my name. I ran against her for mayor some years ago. She still holds a grudge. You probably should have gone to Brad Wilcox. He's the city recorder. He'll have all the names."

"I went to Mr. Wilcox's house."

"And he didn't help you?"

"No. He just said he wasn't at liberty to share public records."

"I guess I can understand that. He probably thought you were a serial killer."

"No, that was the mayor. Wilcox thought I was a crazed stalker."

Ray grinned. "Well, it's not like anyone in town is private. I mean, pretty much everyone's listed in the local phone book."

I looked at him blankly. "Midway has a phone book?"

"Of course. Doesn't every city have a phone book?"

I felt stupid for not having thought of that. "A phone book would be helpful."

"I'm sure we've got a few extra lying around. Would you like me to find you one?"

"Yes, please."

Ray walked up to the front counter. He returned carrying a small directory printed on newsprint. "Here you go, sir. I should have just given you that to begin with. Probably would have saved you some humiliation."

I took the book from him and examined the cover.

The Park City / Heber Valley phone book
Comprising Summit & Wasatch Counties

The directory was about the size of a trade paperback novel. I thumbed through it, then set it down. "This is just what I need. Thank you."

"My pleasure. I have one question for you."

"Yes?"

"I'm assuming you're going to come up with a list of possible residents to visit. So, when you visit these people, what are you going to say to them?"

Dale's dilemma. "I'm not sure."

"Well, you might find that you need to be a little sneaky. If you tell them that you're trying to find someone from the Internet, they might close up. Especially if she's the *one*. You know what I mean?"

"What do you mean by 'sneaky'?"

"Well, maybe you tell them that you're with the US Census."

"They'd believe that?"

"I would think so. I would."

I thought a moment. "I don't know. I think I'd rather be straightforward."

"I'm not telling you how to conduct your hunt," he said, pushing back his chair, "just giving some advice. Good luck finding your woman. I'd better get on home to my own before she puts out a missing-persons report. Is there anything else I can do for you?"

"There's one thing," I said. "Please don't take this wrong, the food here is delicious but a bit . . ."

"You would like a recommendation of somewhere to eat besides the inn."

"If you wouldn't mind."

"Of course I wouldn't mind. We've got the usual fast food haunts, which I would *not* recommend. I would recommend the Mistletoe Diner. It's just off Main Street, only a few blocks from the Midway community center, near the city offices. You probably drove past it this afternoon."

"Food's good?"

"Food's excellent."

"Thanks. I'll give it a try."

"Oh, and if Thelma makes pie, eat it." Ray stood and walked out of the room.

Just a minute after he left my waiter brought out my meal. "Here you are, sir. *Bon appétit.*"

After dinner I carried the phone book up to my room. I sat on my bed and began thumbing through its pages. The first two-thirds of the book were yellow-paged business listings. I turned to the white pages and leafed through it until I found where *H* began. There were six pages of last names that began with the letter *H*.

I took a pen from the nightstand and began going down the pages. There were two columns on each side, with about a hundred listings in each column. There were only a few names with the middle name or initial of *B*, but I didn't want to rule out the rest.

Many of the listings were men or residents of Park City, which disqualified them. By the time I was done, I was left with a list of eighteen names.

Hall, Leslie B.
Hanks, Linda
Harding, Linda
Hardy, Liz
Harkness, Lori

Harman, Lindsey
Heger, Laurie
Henrie, Lillian
Heughs, Layla
Hewitt, Lisa
Hickman, Leah
Higham, Louise
Hill, Lorraine
Hitesman, Laurel
Holbrook, Lilly
Howard, Lydia
Howell, Lisa
Hoyt, LaDawn

I was making progress. At least I had a list. Tomorrow morning I would start my search at the top, with Leslie Hall.

Chapter

Sixteen

Breakfast the next morning was eggs Blackstone. The difference between eggs Blackstone and eggs Benedict is the former is made with bacon instead of ham. It was delicious, as were the apple fritter pancakes. I expected to run into Ray in the dining room but he never came by.

After breakfast I went for a brisk two-mile walk along the road next to the golf course, then came back to my room and showered. There was a text from Nate. As usual, he was succinct.

How goes it?

I texted back.

The hunt has just begun. I've narrowed LBH down to 18 leads.

He texted back.

Seek and destroy.

After I had dressed, I sat down and looked at my list again. I wasn't sure how long it would take to visit eighteen people, but unless LBH was, coincidentally, the last name on my list, I wouldn't need to visit them all.

I grabbed Ray's map and walked out to my car with the list. My windshield was iced over, so I brushed the snow off with my arm, then, using a credit card, attempted to scrape off the ice. A man in the parking lot next to me was also scraping the snow from his SUV. He watched me with amusement. After a moment he approached.

"Don't you have a scraper?" he asked.

"No."

"Stand aside." He scraped, then brushed the snow off my windows. After he finished he said, "You're going to need to pick up a scraper."

"Thanks. Do you know where I can find one?"

"Anywhere. Grocery stores, gas stations."

I thanked him again and he walked back to his car. I got inside and started my car. As I waited for it to heat up, I looked at the first name on my list. Leslie B. Hall. 1219 Montreux Circle.

"All right, Leslie. Let's see if you're the one."

I typed her address into my phone's GPS. This time it came up with a location. The house was about a half mile from the Swiss Center, but if Swiss Days attracted thousands of people, it was conceivable that people would still be parking out that far. Leslie could be the one.

Leslie Hall's house was modest and set back from the street. The front walkway hadn't yet been shoveled. There was a snow-covered refurbished

John Deere tractor in the driveway with a *For Sale* sign taped to its engine.

I had not prepared for the snow. Wearing just loafers, I trudged through shin-deep snow up the walk and cautiously climbed the stairs to a wooden porch, which creaked a bit beneath me. I pushed the doorbell but didn't hear anything, so I knocked. Just seconds later a well-fed man holding a can of Budweiser opened the door.

"What can I do you for?" the man asked.

"Sorry to bother you, but I'm looking for Leslie Hall."

He looked at me narrowly then said, "Well, you found me."

"You're Leslie?"

"That's what it says on my driver's license. Who you expecting?"

"Sorry. I must have the wrong address."

"You were expecting a woman, weren't you? I know. I get it all the time."

"You're right. My mistake."

His eyes narrowed. "You one of them bounty hunters?"

"Me? No."

"Salesman?"

"No. Well, I mean, I am, but that's not why I'm here. I'm just looking for someone I met on the Internet."

The corners of his mouth rose in a knowing smile. "Ah, yeah. I get it. She blew you off, huh? Gave you a bad address, wrong name?"

I nodded, deciding it would be easier to go with his theory than my real story. "Wouldn't be the first time."

"I know how you feel, buddy. Happens to me *all* the time. I meet a hot babe at a bar, she gives me her address, I drive to it, blammo, it's a freakin' landfill or a church parking lot, you know what I mean? Happens all the time. Women are ruthless."

"They can be. You have a good day."

"You too. I didn't catch your name."

"Alex."

"Alex, Leslie. Guess you know that already."

"Yeah, thanks, Leslie. Sorry to bother you."

"No worries."

As I walked away he shouted after me, "Hey, there's a Jazz game on tonight if you're not busy. Playin' the Trailblazers. Cold brew, game, could be fun."

I turned back. "Thank you. But I have work to do."

"She really broke your heart, didn't she? I tell you, nothing eases woman pain like a little bromanship."

"Thanks. I'll think about it."

"Game starts at seven. I'll put some brats on."

"I'll think about it. Thanks."

I heard the home's door shut behind me as I walked back to my car.

Interesting people.

Chapter
Seventeen

The next name on my list was Linda Hanks. Her house was only a few blocks from where the Swiss Days festivities were held, so it could potentially be the place. The real LBH. And I'd never met a man named Linda.

The house, a one-level bungalow with a small front yard, was covered in olive-green wood paneling with an orange door and orange trim around the windows. Pink plastic flamingos stood breast-high in the snow. A white Subaru wagon was parked in the driveway.

I parked in the street, near the mailbox, and walked up the concrete driveway to the shoveled sidewalk that led to the front door.

I rang the doorbell and the door opened almost immediately, catching me off guard. An attractive blond woman stood in the threshold. "That was fast. I just barely hung up with your office. Come in, please. It's in the kitchen."

"Excuse me?" I said.

"Hurry, it's getting all over."

She turned her back to me and rushed toward the dining area. I hesitated for a moment, then followed. The kitchen's linoleum floor was covered with water and I could hear running water over the sound of the grinding of a garbage disposal.

"I don't know what happened. I just turned on the disposal and just a few seconds later water started shooting all over. I shut the cupboard door but it keeps coming out." She looked as distressed as she sounded, so much so that I didn't have the heart to tell her that I wasn't the plumber. At any rate, what better chance to discover LBH? She certainly fit the criteria.

"Just a minute," I said, crouching down in front of the sink. I took off my coat, then opened the cupboard door, catching a splash of water in my face. I saw the problem right away. The black plastic pipe connected to the disposal had slipped off.

"Could you turn the disposal off, please?"

"Yes, sorry." She reached over the counter and turned off a switch. The grinding stopped.

I lifted the pipe and slipped it back over the disposal and the water stopped spraying. I pushed it in as tight as I could but still needed to adjust the clamp. "Do you have a flathead screwdriver?"

"I . . ." Her brow fell. "Didn't you bring tools?"

"I don't want to let go of this. May I use yours?"

"What kind of screwdriver?"

"The kind with a flat end."

"Just a minute." She returned with three different sizes of screwdrivers. I took the largest of the three, loosened the clamp, then slid the hose clamp over the outer pipe and tightened it until the pipe indented under its pressure. I climbed out from under the sink and handed her back the screwdriver. She had calmed, and I was finally able to get a good look at her. She was maybe a few years older than me, pretty, with thick blond hair pulled back in a ponytail. She wore skinny jeans and a red sweater.

"That should hold."

"Thank you," she said. "Now I just have to mop this up. You'd think that after being single for three years I'd know something about plumbing."

"I really don't know that much myself," I said. "Just enough to get by."

She gave me a peculiar look. "I thought you had to pass a test or something to be a plumber."

It took me a moment to process her confusion. "Right. Of course. You know what they say, the more you know, the more you know you don't know."

She looked even more confused but said, "How much do I owe you?"

The question caught me off guard. "I'll send you a bill."

"Okay. How much was it? So I can plan on it."

"Ten dollars," I said.

"Just ten dollars? Your receptionist said the house call was a minimum fifty dollars."

"That's the normal price, but I was driving by the neighborhood, so no problem. If you could just write down your name for me, I'll have the office take care of this."

"Oh," she said. "That explains why you didn't have any tools."

"Right. And that's also why I don't have an invoice. My apologies."

"No problem."

She retrieved a pad and pen, then wrote in a distinctly feminine scrawl:

Linda Hanks

"Is that your full legal name?" I asked.

"No, sorry." I watched as she wrote her name again.

Linda Wells Hanks

I looked at it with disappointment. "Is that your maiden name? Wells?"

"Yes. I still use my ex's last name. Actually, my middle name is Michelle."

I folded up the paper. "Thank you."

"No, thank you. I feel guilty only paying you ten dollars. I really should pay you back somehow. Would it be inappropriate for me to invite you to dinner?" I noticed that she furtively glanced at my bare ring finger. "I mean, if you're available."

I hesitated for a moment, then said, "Of course. That would be nice."

"What are you doing tomorrow night?"

"I should be free."

"Wonderful. Seven o'clock?"

"I'll have to check my schedule, but I'll give you a call."

"Sure." She wrote down her phone number and followed me to the door. She watched me walk to my car, then waved as I drove away.

Just halfway down the block I passed a truck wrapped with a picture of a drain and the words *Linton Plumbing* written on the side. I thought of driving back and intercepting him, but I wasn't sure what I'd say, so I just kept on. Dinner plans with Linda probably weren't going to work out.

Chapter

Eighteen

Two down, sixteen to go. I looked at my list. The next name was also a Linda. Linda Harding. I glanced down at my phone to check the time. It was a little past two and I had a text message from my boss. There had been a problem with my client in Oakland, and even though the next home on my list was just three blocks away, I decided to go back to the inn to take care of it.

It was past four before I went back out. I drove directly to the house, a small, white brick rambler. The roof was covered in snow and icicles, some reaching all the way to the ground to form columns. The only color was from the pale-blue front door and the red alarm-system signs poking up through the snow like crocuses.

There was an opened bag of ice melt next to the front door and blue pebbles of snowmelt (I now knew what it was) were scattered about, crunching beneath my feet.

I rang the doorbell and a chime went off inside. A moment later I heard the scuffle of something across the floor, then there was the slide of a chain lock followed by a dead bolt. The door slowly opened.

The woman in the doorway looked to be at least in her late eighties, with gray-white hair. She was leaning against a walker. "May I help you?"

"I'm sorry," I said. "I must have the wrong address."

"What address were you looking for?"

I wasn't sure how to reply. "Actually, this one."

"Well, who are you looking for? I know about everyone in this city. I've been here my whole life."

"Linda Harding?"

"That's me. I'm Linda."

"Yes," I said, still not sure where to go with this. "Actually, the Linda I was looking for was supposed to be a bit . . . younger."

"I'm sorry, I can't oblige you there. I would if I could. I am the only Linda Harding in Midway. Perhaps I could be of assistance. You can tell me more over some hot cocoa. Please come inside."

"No, I've taken enough of your time."

"Time is all I have," she said. "At least what's left of it. And, truthfully, I'm a bit lonely today. I'm sure a fine-looking man like you doesn't know what that feels like, but please, come in. I insist."

She looked at me with such eagerness that I couldn't refuse. Especially someone lonely. "Sure, I have a few minutes," I finally said.

She clapped her hands with delight. "Wonderful."

I stepped inside. The home's interior was out-dated but immaculate and smelled of menthol and lavender. The floor was carpeted in vibrant blue shag and the walls were baby blue with bright white gold leaf on the wainscoting.

All around the house were pictures—framed photographs of families and youth, presumably her children and grandchildren.

"When you rang I was about to put some pop-overs in the oven. I love a good popover, don't you? Especially with a little marmalade. Now I have someone to share them with. Just shut the door behind you." She lightly waddled as she pushed her walker to her kitchen. "Have a seat at the table while I make us some cocoa. I like mine extra chocolaty—how about you?"

"However you make it is fine," I said.

"Fine, fine." She was gone for nearly ten minutes while I sat there looking over her dining room. There were more photographs—some, I presumed, of my hostess in her youth.

She came back without her walker, hunched over and carrying two steaming mugs. "It's a little hot." She set them both down on the table and sat down across from me. "I haven't seen you before. Are you new to Midway?"

"I'm not from here. I'm from Florida."

"Oh, yes. I went to Florida once. My parents took me when I was a little girl. I saw the Okefenokee swamp. Never forgot that. Those alligators were something. They were feeding them chickens. No alligators in Utah. Maybe in the Hogle Zoo, but not running around. It's too cold. I guess the cold's good for something."

"It's definitely cold."

"Don't let that be a deterrent to moving here, if that's your inclination. The weather may be cold but the people are warm. Most of them, anyway. Here in Midway, we like to look after each other. The boy across the street comes and shovels and salts my driveway whenever it snows . . ."

For the next sixty minutes Linda espoused the virtues of life in Heber and Midway while teaching me the towns' 156-year history. She told me that Midway was renamed from "Mound City," after the relocation of an Indian tribe forced the building of a fort midway between the towns of Heber and Mound City, hence Midway.

There was just one break from the conversation, when the timer on the oven sounded and Linda brought out a tray of hot popovers, orange marmalade, and raw honey.

She finally came back to the purpose of my visit. "Now, this other Linda Harding you're looking for, could it be that you have the wrong Midway? You know, there are at least a dozen cities named Midway in this country, including the famous Midway Island, which marked a turning point in World War II. My great-uncle Kirby was in the Navy. He was stationed at Midway—not this Midway, the island in the Pacific, Midway—when the war began. That's where the Japanese—"

Realizing that we were potentially entering another hourlong lecture, I quickly stood. "Ms. Harding?"

"Linda, please, Alex. Call me Linda. Why are you standing? Do you need to use the washroom?"

"No, but I think you may be right. I might be in the wrong city, and I'd better get right on this while there's still time. Thank you so much for the cocoa and popovers and your company."

"The cocoa and popovers were certainly no trouble, and I'm always so glad for company. As a matter of fact, I'm just about to start making dinner. Would you like to stay? You have to eat."

"Thank you so much, but I have other commitments I need to attend to. And thank you so much for setting me straight. I'll see myself to the door."

I headed to the front door with Linda still talking behind me. "I would love to have you for dinner. It's no trouble."

When I opened the door it was already dark outside, the curtain of evening accented by a softly falling snow. "Thank you, but I'd really better get on my way."

"Come back soon," she said. "Tomorrow I'm baking my cinnamon pull-aparts."

As peculiar as my first day of visits had been, outside of the two city bureaucrats, everyone

I'd met so far had wanted to spend more time with me. I had come away with three dinner invitations. *What if the world's best-kept secret was that the whole world was lonely?*

I was able to clear some of the snow off my windshield with the wipers but had to use my hands for the rest, leaving them wet and cold. On Main Street I found a convenience store. There was a box of snow brush/scrapers near the front door and I bought the largest size they had.

In spite of Mrs. Harding's popovers, I was hungry, so I decided to find the restaurant that Ray had told me about. The Mistletoe Diner.

Chapter
Nineteen

I drove cautiously, my wipers flailing wildly against the increasingly steady snowfall as I looked for the diner. I had the car's defroster on full, which had cleared patches of windshield about the size of two large pizzas but not all of it, which is partially why I drove past the diner twice before finally finding it, a block and a half east of the Midway community center.

Unlike most of the other establishments on the street, the diner didn't look Swiss. It also didn't have much going on by way of signage. The *Mistletoe Diner* on the neon sign above the front door didn't light—only a sprig of green mistletoe that moved back and forth, looking more like a feather duster than holiday-themed foliage.

The diner was built adjacent to the road and was long and narrow, with a curtained window at each booth along the front of the building. The windows glowed invitingly.

I parked my car, then walked inside. Hanging directly above the waiting area was a sprig of dusty mistletoe that looked a few decades old. Christmas music was softly playing. *Bing Crosby.* I wondered if, considering the diner's name, there was always Christmas music playing.

"Someone will be right with you," an older

woman said as she walked past me to a table. She was wearing a white apron over a black shirt with the sleeves rolled up. She said to a younger woman on the far end of the front counter, "Ari, will you help the gentleman?"

"Of course." The waitress had been facing away from me and she turned, wiping her hands on her apron. "Hi. Welcome to the Mistletoe Diner."

The young woman was dressed the same as the other waitress, with a white apron and black blouse, except her blouse was short-sleeved, exposing the pale, smooth flesh of her arms. Her dark-brown hair softly cradled her face. She had lush lips and full, high, defined cheeks that almost seemed to crowd her dark eyes.

The truth is, most of the time when we meet someone it barely registers a memory—you know, those times when someone tells us their name and we forget it before we even use it. Then there are times that some force, invisible as magnetic waves, creates an immediate pull and connection. The latter describes the first moment I saw *her*. She was attractive, which in itself implies some form of magnetism, but it was more than that. If she was beautiful, she also looked, like the diner, a little worn down and frayed around the edges. Peculiarly, there was something familiar about her.

I was so busy taking her in that it almost startled me when she spoke.

"Dinner for one?" she asked softly, grabbing a menu from the front counter.

"Yes. It's just me." *Why was I always embarrassed to say that?*

"Would you like a table or a booth?"

"Booth," I said, adding, "I'm a recluse."

She gently smiled and it was warm and pretty. "The isolation booth it is."

I followed her to the back corner of the diner. "Here you are. Seclusion."

"Thank you." I sat and she handed me a menu.

"My name is Aria. Can I get you something to drink?"

"That's a pretty name," I said.

She lightly smiled and pulled back a strand of hair from her face. "Thank you. I had nothing to do with choosing it. Would you like something to drink?"

"Do you have lemonade?"

"Yes. We have Minute Maid. I can put some strawberry or blackberry syrup in it if you like."

"Strawberry, please."

"One strawberry lemonade. I'll give you a minute to look over the menu."

I watched her walk back to the kitchen, then opened my menu. The food selection was typical of a diner: chicken-fried steak, mashed potatoes, that sort of thing. I was still perusing the menu when she returned carrying my drink and a basket of bread. "Here you are, your drink and some bread. Did you have time to decide on what you'd like?"

"I'm still undecided. What do you like?"

She leaned comfortably against the opposite vinyl backrest. "I usually order the chicken pot pie."

I set down my menu. "That sounds good. I'll have that."

"We're out of it tonight." When I looked at her blankly she said, "You asked me what I like, not what we have."

I smiled. "Fair enough. What do you like that you *have?*"

"I would recommend the meat loaf. Or the sage-roasted chicken. They're both good."

"And you're sure that you have both?"

She grinned slightly. "I'm pretty sure we do. And I also recommend the split pea soup, if you like split pea soup. If you don't, then don't order it."

"I'll have the meat loaf and a cup of the soup."

"The meat loaf comes with mashed potatoes with mushroom gravy and corn or mixed vegetables."

"What kind of vegetables?"

She thought. "It's mostly corn too."

I laughed again. "I'll have that."

"All right, that'll be just a few minutes. Would you like your soup first?"

"Yes."

"Oh, and enjoy the bread. I baked it this morning."

She disappeared back into the kitchen. I tasted my lemonade, then stirred in the strawberry syrup that had settled to the bottom of the glass. As I sipped my drink I panned the dining room.

Some modern diners try to mimic traditional old-time diners with faux vintage Coke signs, vinyl bar chairs, and neon clocks, accessories now more likely to be made in China than Toledo, Ohio. But the accessories surrounding me were old and authentic, as if the place were caught in a time warp. And the other patrons seemed as eclectic as the diner itself: truck drivers, old folks out for pie, tourists.

Aria returned carrying my soup steaming in a porcelain bowl on a matching plate. "Here you are. The soup du jour. Be careful, it's hot."

"That was fast."

"It doesn't take long to ladle soup into a bowl." She set the bowl down in front of me. "I'll be back with the rest of your meal in a few minutes."

I tried the soup and was pleased to find that it was as good as anything I'd had in my travels. Per Aria's suggestion, I took a piece of thick white bread, buttered it, and took a bite. It was good as well. I broke some pieces of the bread into the bowl and began to eat.

I had just finished the soup when Aria returned carrying my meal and a fresh lemonade, even though I had drunk less than half of what I had.

"Here you are. How was the soup?" She looked at my empty bowl. "It must not be terrible."

"I could probably force down another bowl."

"I think you'll like this as well." She set down a platter with meat loaf and a generous helping of mashed potatoes covered with brown gravy. That's when I noticed the small diamond on her ring finger. Peculiarly, it bothered me.

"Can I get you anything else?"

"No. Thank you."

"Just wave if you need anything." She walked across the room to a new booth of diners.

She moved gracefully. She was in a small-town diner, but she was not without poise. I suspected that she could have been in one of the finest restaurants in Europe and won the crowd. I wondered if she was from the town or a transplant.

I ate slowly, in no particular hurry to be anywhere. I tried not to stare at her. I saw her glancing over at me several times, though I'm sure she was just doing her job. As I was finishing she came over to check on me.

"How's your dinner?"

"I'm glad you recommended the meat loaf."

"Comfort food," she said. "Perfect for a cold winter night."

I desperately scrambled for something to keep the conversation going. "I sounded a little weird telling you that I'm a recluse. I'm not, like, Howard Hughes."

"A lot of people don't like company when they eat. I used to have a dog who wouldn't eat if you looked at him."

"You just compared me to your dog."

She smiled again, and it was beautiful. "At least he was a *cute* dog."

I laughed. *Was she flirting?*

"It surprises me that most of the truck drivers want to be alone. You would think that being on the road all the time would make them want company, but I think it does the opposite. Most of them shun it. At least when they come here."

"I think I understand," I said. "I travel a lot for work. It seems that the more I travel, the more I just want to stay inside my hotel room and order room service. It happens."

She thought a moment, then said, "Maybe we get out of the habit of being around people faster than we think." She took a deep breath and smiled. "That got deep, fast."

I put out my hand. "By the way, my name is Alex."

"Hi, Alex. What brings you to Midway?"

"How do you know I'm not from Midway?"

She cocked her head. "Because if you were, I would have already known you."

"I'm from Daytona Beach, Florida."

"The beach. It's been so long since I've seen

beach. And sand. And warmth. They say there's four seasons in Utah. Almost winter, winter, still winter, and road construction."

"There's a lot of snow out there."

She looked out the window. "It's still coming down."

I shook my head. "It's relentless. Are the roads safe?"

She unsuccessfully hid her amusement. "Is it your first time in snow?"

"It's my first time driving in snow."

"Just don't drive too fast. We're supposed to get a lot more snow this week. We get, like, a hundred inches a year. How long are you here?"

"I'm not sure. About a week."

"What is it that you do?"

"I sell software that counts cars."

"Why would someone want to do that?"

"For a lot of reasons. Traffic control. Safety."

She nodded. "Government stuff."

"Exactly."

"Where are you staying?"

"At the Blue Boar Inn."

"The Blue Boar is really nice," she said. "I've never stayed there, but I've had dinner there. It's a lot fancier than the diner."

"The innkeeper there recommended your diner."

"Ray," she said. "He's sweet. He comes here every Thursday for pie. On Thursdays Thelma makes pecan pie just for him. Speaking of which, would you like some pie? Tonight we have Thelma's caramel apple pie."

"Ray warned me not to pass on any pie," I said. "So yes, please."

"Would you like cheese with that?"

"Cheese with pie?"

"You know what they say, apple pie without the cheese is like a kiss without a squeeze."

"I've never heard that."

"Maybe it's a small-town thing. Being from Florida, you're probably more of a Key lime pie kind of guy, anyway."

"I love Key lime pie."

"Why wouldn't you?" She glanced over at the counter, where a man was looking at us. I couldn't tell for sure but it looked like he was glowering at me.

"I need to check on my other tables, then I'll get your pie. I'll hurry."

As she walked away I was again struck by how familiar she looked. *Where did I know her from?*

Five minutes later she returned with the pie. It was lattice-topped and the crust was lightly browned and encrusted with sugar.

"It's a work of art," I said.

"Thelma is to pie what Michelangelo was to sculpture," she said. "And here's your check."

I looked it over. "May I add something to my bill? I'd like to take some pie back to Ray. To thank him for the recommendation."

"I'll get the pie. Don't worry about it. Just tell him Aria says hi."

"Thank you."

She went over and poured coffee to a man at a booth, then disappeared into the kitchen while I ate my pie. Thelma was indeed a pie-making genius.

When Aria returned I gave her my credit card. She took care of the bill and brought me my receipt. I left her a large tip. "It was nice meeting you, Alex," she said. "I hope you'll come back in before you leave town."

"I'm sure I will. Pecan pie is my favorite."

"Thursday," she said. "She makes it on Thursday."

As I walked out to my car I didn't mind the cold. I started up the car, turned on its heater, grabbed my new snow scraper, and cleaned the snow off the windshield. In spite of making little progress with LBH, I felt happy. I don't think it was because of the pie.

Chapter
Twenty

The next morning at breakfast Ray stopped by my table. "Good morning, my friend. How goes the hunt?"

"It goes," I said. "I'm glad you're here. I have something for you."

"You do?" he said, sitting down.

I handed him the Styrofoam box with the piece of pie. He opened it and smiled. "Oh, yes. Thelma's caramel apple pie. Food of the gods."

"I had the kitchen refrigerate it overnight."

"Did you have some for yourself?"

"Yes."

"Then you know Thelma's genius. You should try Thelma's pecan," he said. "That's worth writing home about." He grabbed a fork from another table and began to eat. Then he looked up at me. "So you found the diner."

"It was as good as you said. And the pie's courtesy of Aria."

A pleasant look came across his face. "Better yet, you found *Aria*." He put a special emphasis on her name. "If I were younger . . ."

"So you like Aria?"

"*Like? Adulate* or *worship* are better words. Did she say anything about me?"

"She sent the pie and said to say hi."

"That's it?"

"She also called you 'sweet.' "

He frowned. "Sweet. Like a puppy. That's the problem with age. You're cute, not sexy."

"It's just as well," I said, hiding my amusement. "You're married."

"Yes, I am. Very, very married."

"As is she."

He took another bite of pie then looked up. "No, Aria's not married."

"She had a ring."

"I know. That's truck driver repellent. She *was* married. When she first came to Midway. But that was a long time ago."

"She's not from Midway?"

"No, she's a transplant. She came here about six years ago. She and her husband, Wayne, Wade, Walt, something with a *W*, started a coffee shop, but it didn't make it. He left, she stayed. That pretty much sums it up."

"She's been alone since?"

"Yes, it's a wonder. Beautiful girl like that. Beautiful inside and out. One of those rare women who are beautiful but don't know it." He thought a moment then said, "I think Polish girls are like that. The whole country." He looked up at me. "Not like the Midway men leave her alone. They don't. The problem is, the young ones are all married, and the guys . . . well, we're not really in the running, are we?"

"I'm sure you would be if you weren't already taken."

"Now you're being unctuous."

I grinned. "Where is she from?"

"Minnesota, I think." He took another bite of pie. "Yes, Minnesota. She doesn't talk much about her life before Midway." He leaned back and his voice softened. "I worry about her, though. I worry about her a lot."

"Why is that?"

"She has eyes of sadness. Deep, deep sadness. It's pretty, in a way—vulnerability can be pretty. But hers . . ." He sighed. "Every year the light in her eyes is a little less bright. I wonder if someday the candle will just flicker and go out." He took a deep breath. "Loneliness gets to you. You know what I mean?"

His words filled me with sadness. "I do."

We briefly languished in the moment, then Ray took another bite of pie and said, "Well, onward, right? Did you make use of the phone book I gave you?"

"Yes. I made a list of all the LHs in the area. I came up with eighteen possible candidates."

"Do you have the list with you?"

"Yes." I pulled the list from my pocket, unfolded it, and handed it to him. He smoothed it out against the table, looked at it for a moment, then took out a pen.

"Okay, the first name here on your list, Leslie Hall, is not a woman."

"That would have been good to know yesterday."

He looked up at me. "You went and visited old Les?"

"Old Les? Yes."

Ray smiled. "How did that go?"

"Awkward. But he did invite me over for brats and a basketball game."

"His wife left him last year. Took their two kids and ran off with a lawyer from Salt Lake City." He looked back down at my list. "Don't know about the second name here. But Linda Harding, she's older. Probably wouldn't know how to turn the computer on, but sweet as divinity."

"Yes, I met her. Had a long talk." I sat back. "Those three were pretty much my day yesterday. I should have shown you this first. Would you mind going through the rest of it?"

"I would not mind." He ran his pen down the list, occasionally stopping to cross someone out.

~~Hall, Leslie B.~~
~~Hanks, Linda~~
~~Harding, Linda~~
Harman, Lindsey
Hardy, Liz
Harkness, Lori

Heger, Laurie
~~Henrie, Lillian~~
~~Heughs, Layla~~
Hewitt, Lisa
~~Hickman, Leah~~
Higham, Louise
Hill, Lorraine
~~Hitesman, Laurel~~
~~Holbrook, Lilly~~
Howard, Lydia
Howell, Lisa
Hoyt, LaDawn

"You can take Layla Heughs, Leah Hickman, Lilly Holbrook, and Lillian Henrie off your list. Layla and Leah are in their eighties. Lilly and Lillian are in their nineties. In fact, Lilly might have passed last month." He thought for a moment then said, "Yes, she passed.

"Laurel Hitesman is hot and heavy on the golf pro over at the Homestead Resort and has a boyfriend in Connecticut, so I don't think she's your lonely woman."

I wondered how he knew so much about these people, but didn't ask.

"I think LaDawn's in her fifties. She's still a possibility. She's a checker over at Ridley's, the grocery store off Main Street. She's well preserved. She does a lot of yoga and stuff."

"That leaves just ten people," I said.

He handed me back the list. "Ten people out of an entire city. That's not bad. You could do that in a couple more days."

"Then I best get at it."

"Yes, you best," he said. He closed the container around his pie and stood. "I hope you don't mind if I take this with me."

"Of course not."

He started to turn, then stopped and looked back at me. "And Alex?"

"Yes, sir."

"When you see Aria again, thank her for the pie."

"What makes you think I'll see her again?"

He slightly leaned forward. "You noticed that she had a ring." He winked at me, then turned and walked away. After he was gone I laughed to myself. *Smart man.*

After I finished breakfast, I went upstairs to gather my things, then went back out into the cold to find LBH.

Chapter

Twenty-one

It didn't take me long to find my first stop. Lindsey Harman. Her redbrick house, with its white gingerbread trim under the eaves, was picturesque, looking more like one of the Swiss-themed stores along Midway's Main Street than a private residence. In keeping with the season, it was strung with red and white Christmas lights matching the Swiss-themed elements as well as bestowing a festive holiday feel to the façade.

The house was close enough to the fairgrounds that LBH would have definitely seen a lot of festival attendees. There was a *For Sale* sign in front, which would also make sense, since she was planning on moving back home.

I walked up to the front door. There was no doorbell, so I knocked. Nothing. I knocked again. After a few minutes without any response, I walked around the side of the house and knocked on a side door. Still no answer.

I walked back to my car and made a notation on my list to return later on. Then I drove on to find the next candidate, Liz Hardy.

This next house was only a few blocks from the first but not nearly as nice. It was dated and looked to be made of old, handmade bricks— the large kind with thick mortar between them. Its snow-laden shake roof peaked in the middle of the house, above the front door, which was beneath a small second-floor balcony with a door opening out of it. There were white shutters and finials over the windows.

The door opened slowly. "Yes?" The man was slightly shorter than me and a few years older. He wore a sweater and thick-rimmed glasses.

"Hi. My name is Alex, I'm looking for Liz Hardy."

"You are?" he said with a condescending tone. "You're looking for Liz."

His response baffled me. "Yes, sir."

"And how do you know *Elizabeth?*"

"From the Internet."

"Is that so?"

"Yes, sir. I've been following her blog."

He just continued to gaze at me with the same peculiar expression, then he said, "All right. Just a minute. I'll get her."

He walked back into the house, returning a moment later carrying a bright copper urn. "Here she is. What would you like to say to her?"

I stood there looking at him. "She's where?"

"Here," he said, holding out the urn. "She's in here."

I couldn't decide which was worse, that he was joking or that he wasn't. Either way, it was time to leave.

"Sorry for your loss," I said. I turned and walked quickly back to my car, almost slipping on a patch of ice. *Interesting people.*

Chapter
Twenty-two

The fact that the next house had at least a dozen *No Trespassing* and *No Solicitation* signs and the welcome mat said *GO AWAY* should have been clues enough to stay away. Whoever lived here clearly wasn't fond of visitors.

I rang the doorbell and a moment later the door opened just a few inches. I could see the eclipsed face of a gaunt, angry woman.

"Why are you on my property?"

"I . . . are you Ms. Harkness?"

"Who are you?"

"I'm with . . . the census. I'm just verifying that you are the occupant of this home."

"You're not with the census."

"I just need to verify your record and I'll be gone. Does your middle name start with a *B*?"

"Show me your identification. Census workers are required to wear identification."

"If you could just . . ."

"You're a fraud!" she screamed. "Show me your ID or I'm calling the police."

"I'm not showing it to you."

"Then I'm calling the police, you pervert. The police chief is a friend of mine, you can tell your story to him." She lifted her phone and pushed a button.

"Look, I'm just . . ."

I could hear the phone ringing on the other end.

"Really? You have the police on speed dial?"

Just then she lifted a bottle of Mace. "Let's see how you like this."

I turned and ran across the snow, catching a whiff of the Mace she sprayed after me.

"Yeah, you better run, you sick perv! I'm taking a picture of your license plate." She ran out after me holding the Mace in one hand and her phone in the other. I hit the gas and gunned my car out of there.

If she was LBH, there was a good reason she was lonely.

Chapter

Twenty-three

After the day's failed visits I was ready to take a break for lunch. It wasn't all failure. At least my list was smaller. I didn't know whether or not Aria worked during the day, but I decided to drop by anyway. The truth was, I'd thought about her all day. The odd thing was, it made me feel sort of guilty—as if I was cheating on LBH.

As I walked into the diner, I saw Aria standing at the front counter ringing up a ticket for a stooped, elderly customer. She glanced over at me and smiled. She looked a little different, less tired, perhaps the difference between the beginning of a shift and the end of one.

As she handed the old man back his change he said, "I'm standing under mistletoe, do I get my kiss?"

"Of course, George. You always get your kiss." Aria walked around the counter and pecked the old man on the cheek. As the man turned toward me I saw the extent of his nearly toothless smile, which was so large I thought it might crack his face in two.

Aria turned to me. "Back already."

I was pleased that she remembered me. "It was the pie."

"The apple pie or the chicken pot pie you didn't get?"

"Both."

"Darn. And I was hoping it was me."

This was flirting, right?

She glanced behind her. "Would you like to sit in the same place?"

"Sure."

"It's . . . Alex?"

She either had a photographic memory or I had made an impression on her. I hoped for the latter. "That's right. And you're Aria."

"Still me." She grabbed a menu. "Follow me, please."

I followed her back to the same booth where I'd sat the day before and sat down. She handed me the menu.

"So, today, we do have our chicken pot pie."

"Then that's what I'll have."

"And, I should warn you, there's just one piece of Thelma's huckleberry pie left. If you think that might be in your future, I can set it aside."

"Set it aside," I said.

"You won't be disappointed." I wondered if I would ever meet Thelma—the pie goddess.

"Strawberry lemonade?"

Maybe she did have a photographic memory. "Just a plain lemonade today."

"Lemonade it is. I'll be right back."

The diner was not as full as it had been at

night, but Aria seemed to be running the floor by herself. As I watched her (I couldn't keep my eyes off of her), I thought about what Ray had said about her eyes of sadness. I could see what he meant. At first I had mistaken them for fatigue, but beneath her constant greetings, I could see something restrained. Something hurt. Like a spiritual fracture.

Aria brought out a lemonade, setting it in front of me. "There you are. So how's your car counting going?"

I gave her a slight grin. "It's interesting."

"Is interesting good or bad?"

"Just not quite how I expected it to go. That's the thing about traffic—you can't always predict how things will work out."

"Does that mean you'll have to stay longer than you expected?"

I liked the question. "It's likely."

She smiled. "I'll be right back."

As a salesman, I prided myself on my ability to read body language, but with this woman I felt illiterate. I really couldn't read whether she was interested in me or she was just the world's greatest waitress. Maybe both were true.

Or, then, maybe I was just an idiot misreading her kindness for flirtation. I'm told that happens a lot with men. I once had a female colleague tell me that she'd stopped smiling at men.

"Why would you do that?" I had asked.

"Because half of them are so hard up that if a decent-looking woman gives them any attention, they mistake it for a come-on."

Was that me?

About ten minutes later Aria walked back to my table, carrying my meal. "There you go, Thelma's famous chicken pot pie. I hope it's worth the wait. Can I get you anything else?"

"I'm good for now."

"I'll be back to check on you in a minute."

Not surprisingly, it was excellent. I hadn't realized that Thelma had her magical hands in the chicken pot pie too.

When Aria came back I was ready for her.

"How's the pie?"

"Worth the wait."

"Good. Let me know if I can get you anything else."

She was about to leave when I took the leap. "I wanted to ask you, in the event that I do have to stay longer, is there anything to do in Midway?"

"There's a lot to do here," she said. "Not a lot compared to, say, New York or Paris, or even Florida, but there are things worth seeing."

"What kind of things?"

"Have you seen the ice castle?"

"What's that?"

"It's a castle made entirely of ice. The artist made it using something like twenty million pounds of ice. It has tunnels and caverns and

193

archways of solid ice. Then he puts lights inside it. It looks like something out of a fairy tale. People come from all over the country to see it."

"You just walk through it?"

"Yes. I mean, there's a fee. It's like ten dollars."

"Do many people go?"

"The paper said that more than a quarter million people go through it each year. It's almost getting to where you need a reservation."

"What happens when the weather gets warm?"

An amused smile crossed her face. "It melts."

I laughed. "Maybe I'll go see it tonight. How late is it open?"

"I think they close up around ten. But one of the managers is a diner here. He said that if I wanted to go later he would let me in the back way. I'm sure he wouldn't mind. Just ask for Craig."

"Why don't you come with me?"

She didn't reply and I suddenly thought that I really had read her wrong. *How could I have been so obtuse?* I hadn't even planned on asking her right then, the words had just kind of leapt out of my mouth. Now they were hanging awkwardly in the air between us. I wished I could call them back but it was too late. There was nowhere to go but forward. "Would you like to come with me?"

Suddenly her look of surprise gave way to a pleasant smile. "Yes. I'd like that."

Now I was the surprised one. It took me a

moment to recover. "What time do you get off work?"

"Usually around ten. But I'll ask Valerie if she can close for me. If she can, I could leave around nine thirty." She glanced around, then said, "I'll let you know before you go. I better take care of my other tables." She walked off.

We didn't talk much after that, even when she brought me the huckleberry pie. When I walked up to the counter to pay, Aria came up to check me out. "Sorry, I got busy. Valerie says she can close."

"Great," I said, handing her my credit card. After she ran it I said, "So I'll see you at nine thirty."

"Nine thirty," she repeated. I turned to go when she said, "Alex."

"Yes?"

"It's ice. And it's night. Do you have another coat?"

I looked down at my jacket then back at her. "No. Just this."

"You should probably get a real one."

"This isn't a real coat?"

"It's ice," she said again. "And it's night." With a smile, she returned to the floor.

She was right, of course. With the exception of my time at the inn, even with my car's heater blasting, I'd pretty much been cold since I arrived in Utah. Like, chilled-to-the-bone cold. I planned on spending the first week back in Florida just thawing out.

I called the inn to see where I could find a coat. Lita told me that I'd have to go to Park City, which was only about twenty minutes from Midway.

I found an L.L. Bean outlet store near the Park City off-ramp where I picked out a rust-colored down parka with a hood and faux fur trim. I also bought a pair of their least expensive boots. Even being an outlet store, it wasn't cheap, especially considering that I'd probably never wear either item again.

I went back to the inn to relax for a while, then left around a quarter after nine. When I drove up to the front of the diner, Aria was standing outside, her hands deep in her coat pockets. She walked up to my car, looked inside to make sure it was me, then climbed in.

"I think my fingers are frozen," she said.

"Why didn't you wait inside?" I asked.

"It's okay. I didn't want you to have to come in."

I looked at her quizzically. "Why?"

"I just didn't."

I turned the heat all the way up and pointed the dash vents toward her. She rubbed her hands together in front of the closest vent. "Thank you."

"You're welcome."

She looked at me and remarked, "You got a new coat."

"A *real* coat," I said. "A parka. Just like you told me to."

She smiled. "You'll be glad. It gets so cold at night."

"Which is why you really should have waited inside. What if I'd been in a wreck and didn't come?"

She grinned. "Then the next morning I would be found frozen on the front porch like the Little Match Girl."

"Exactly." I put the car into gear. "So, speaking of freezing, where do we find this ice castle?"

"Just head east." She pointed. "You'll drive about a quarter mile until you see a sign that says Soldier Hollow. Then turn right again. You can't miss it. There will be a lot of cars."

"Hopefully all leaving," I said.

"That's the plan," she said. "To have the castle to ourselves."

The ice castle was even more spectacular than I had expected. We arrived around ten o'clock to a throng of cars and people exiting the field. Following Aria's instructions, I pulled my car up around the back of the exhibit. Someone in a yellow reflective vest came over to stop us, but Aria just waved to him and he smiled and let us through.

As we made our way to the back entrance, Aria told me a little of the history behind the ice castle. The artist or, more aptly, the architect behind the castle was a Utah man named Brent Christensen. His ice creations began one cold winter eight years earlier, when he made them in his backyard for his daughter.

What started out of amusement turned into an obsession that had him pushing the limits of ice creation, trying new things with the medium, and soon building larger and larger structures.

Then he convinced a Midway resort to pay him to build a massive ice exhibit—not as big as the castle we were walking around but larger than anything that he, or anyone else, had built before. The public response was phenomenal and inspired Christensen to build full-size ice castles in different locations around the world. Since then, millions of people had toured his ice constructions in Utah as well as elsewhere, including New York and Edmonton, Canada.

During the daylight hours the ice castle is a striking, glacial blue, but at night it is even more spectacular, lit up by thousands of LED lights embedded in the ice.

It took Aria and me forty-five minutes to move through the structure. Still, as beautiful as our setting was, it wasn't the castle that commanded my attention. Aria was far more beautiful than anything that could be created of crystal and light. Near the end of our tour the lights all went off, leaving us alone in the dark, the ice caverns and walls lit only by moonlight.

"I don't think they know we're still in here," Aria said.

"Now I'm especially glad I got a 'real' coat," I said. "Since we'll probably end up spending the night."

To my surprise, she looked a little nervous. "Do you know how to get out?"

"This way," I said.

"Wait." She took my hand. Her fingers were slim and delicate and her hand felt soft and warm in mine. When we were finally out of the castle I was reluctant to give her hand up.

As we walked back to my car she said, "It's not Daytona Beach, but what did you think?"

"I loved it," I said. "And I guarantee that there will never be one in Daytona Beach."

"That's okay," she said. "No one will ever go surfing in Midway. I'm glad you liked it."

It was late and I wasn't sure what was to come next, only that I didn't want the night to end. "Do you want to get a drink or something?"

"I don't drink."

"I meant a hot chocolate."

"Oh." She smiled. "I don't think anything's open."

"The inn is," I said. "We could go there."

She looked a little hesitant.

"If you don't want to . . ."

"I do, I just . . ."

I suddenly understood her reticence. "We'll stay in the dining room."

She nodded. "Okay. Sorry. I'm just a little old-fashioned that way."

"And I'm a gentleman that way."

She smiled. "A gentleman. I almost forgot what those look like."

As we turned onto the road before the inn, Aria said, "Do you know anything about that statue of the boar?"

"No, but it seemed a little familiar."

"It's a casting of a statue in Florence, Italy. There are replicas of it around the world, including the Butchart Gardens in Victoria, British Columbia. But what's really cool is that the statue can be seen in the movie *Hannibal* and two of the Harry Potter movies."

I looked at her in wonder. "How do you know all this?"

"Ray," she said. "He talks a lot. About the inn."

I grinned. "I hadn't noticed."

I parked the car on the cobbled driveway and led her in. A woman I didn't recognize was standing at the front desk. The dining room was empty, though the lights were still on.

"Is anyone in the kitchen?" I asked.

"No, sir. They've gone home for the night."

"I'd like to make some hot chocolate."

"There's a coffeemaker with a tray of tea and cocoa on the counter in the back of the small dining room."

"Thank you." I grabbed a napkin and a few butter cookies from the tray near the stairway, then Aria and I walked back to a table near a window in the smaller dining area.

I held her chair for her, then walked over to the counter and made two cups of hot cocoa. I brought them over and set both cups on the table.

"It's nice to be on the other side of that," she said.

"Of what?"

"Being served."

I smiled. "Be careful, I think it's too hot."

"It smells good."

"The package said it's mint chocolate." I sat down across from her.

"What time do you have to be at work in the morning?" she asked.

"I'm flexible. How about you?"

"Early," she said.

"Do you work every day?"

"Almost. I'm working a lot more lately because of the holidays."

"Extra Christmas money?"

"No. I mean, yes, I can always use the money, but mostly because the other waitresses have a lot of family things. So I pick up their shifts just to help out."

"That's noble of you."

"I don't know about noble but it works out. It's not like I have much going on. And, added bonus, people tip more during the holidays." She took a sip of her cocoa, then quickly withdrew. "That is hot."

"Sorry." I walked out into the hall and returned with a couple cubes of ice. "May I?"

She nodded and I dropped one of the cubes into her cup, the other in mine. "That should help."

"Thank you."

"Remember that woman who sued McDonald's for millions of dollars because her coffee burned her?" I said.

"Yes. Could I sue you for millions because the cocoa's too hot?"

"Sorry, I don't have millions."

"Me neither."

"So tell me about your name. There's got to be a story behind it."

"It came from my father. He was a musician. He played the violin, second chair for the Minnesota Orchestra."

"So he was good."

"He was very good." She looked at me. "He told me that he named me Aria because an aria is an expressive melody and that's how he wanted me to live life, not as the background beat, not the repetitive harmony, but to create my own song.

"The strange thing is that if you look the word up, it says the meaning has changed through time. Today, an aria is usually a self-contained piece for one voice. That pretty much describes my life." She stirred her cocoa again, then took another small sip. "That's better." After a pause and another sip, she said, "Do you think that our name actually affects who we are in life?"

"There's a name for that theory, you know. It's called nominative determinism."

"That's a little scary that you know that."

"Then I'll really scare you. The famous psycho-analyst Carl Jung said that there's a 'grotesque coincidence between a man's name and his peculiarities' . . . or something like that."

"I'm not scared, I'm impressed," she said.

"I just read a business book about that very thing. It pointed out a study on names and con-cluded that because people tend to gravitate to things that are familiar, we are attracted to things that are similar to our names. One of the examples the study gave was the extraordinarily high number of dentists named Dennis."

"Is that true?"

"It was in the book. The book actually had some funny examples. Such as a famous psychiatrist named Angst."

She laughed. "That's not true."

"And there's a meteorologist named Blizzard, a gynecologist named Dr. Ovary, and my personal favorite was a union leader named Raymond Strike."

She laughed again. "You're making this up."

"I wish I was that clever," I said. "Then, of

course, you have the famous English poet William Wordsworth."

"You've made your point. We are what we are named. And I'm an Aria."

"What does that make me?"

"Alex?" she said. "I've no idea."

I took a long drink of my cocoa. "You mentioned Minnesota. Is that where you're from?"

"Wayzata, Minnesota. It's near Lake Minnetonka."

"Is there snow?"

"Lots and lots of snow."

"That's why it doesn't bother you."

"Yes, I'm used to it. I suppose *acclimated* is the word. The snow *and* the cold. Minnesota is colder than Utah." She shook her head. "In more ways than one."

I wasn't sure how to read her last comment. "How did you end up in Midway?"

She lightly groaned as if the question were painful. "I came here with my husband. My *ex*-husband."

"Ray told me that you had a coffee shop."

"*Had* is right. It was pretty short-lived."

"How did you end up in Midway?"

"Shortly after we got married, my husband's cousin called and said that he was starting a coffee shop in Utah and asked him to come and be a partner in it. He couldn't afford to pay salaries, so we were going to earn sweat equity." She shook her head. "How stupid is that, a coffee shop in Midway, Utah?"

"What's wrong with that?"

"Almost three-quarters of the people in Midway are Mormons. They don't drink coffee."

"Like selling bicycles to fish."

"Exactly."

"Then why Utah?"

"He overthought it. He read some book about how Starbucks was founded and decided that he was going to be the next big thing. He thought he was smarter than everyone else. He started looking for cities with the least competition. He never considered that there was a reason there were fewer coffee shops here. I have to admit that the name of the place was pretty good though. *Brewed Awakening*."

I laughed. "And it was."

"Literally."

"So what happened to the Brewed Awakening?"

"After things started going bad, his cousin blamed it on my husband and said we owed him ten thousand dollars. They got in a big fight. They were punching, throwing coffee cups at each other. One of the customers called the police. They were both arrested. I had to post bail to get my husband out of jail.

"After that, Wade—that's my ex's name—never went back to the coffee shop. For about six months he mostly just slept or watched television or played video games. I was already working full-time at the diner but I had to start taking extra shifts to pay bills.

"Then, one day, Wade had this idea that was going to make us rich. He was going to rent snowmobiles to tourists. I should have been more wary, but the truth was I was just so happy that he was going to do something. He was so excited. I believed in him.

"He needed a hundred thousand dollars to get his business going, something, of course, we didn't have. He found this guy who raised capital. His name was Chad something. Maybe Brown. Wade had met him at the coffee shop.

"Chad said he could get us the money, we just needed to come up with ten percent, up front. Chad looked the part. I mean, he was kind of weird-looking, like, his eyes were close together, like a spider, but he dressed in designer clothes, wore expensive sunglasses, drove a Mercedes, all the trappings, you know?"

I nodded. "I know the type."

"So he took us to a nice restaurant. Actually, here. Chad told us, 'If you want to *live* big, you have to *dream* big.' Then he said that the reason most businesses fail wasn't because they weren't a good idea, but because of undercapitalization. So we should go for at least a quarter million. If we gave him just ten percent up front, he'd get us the money. I said, 'We don't have that kind of money.' He said, 'No problem—just take out a loan, and you can pay it back with the money

I raise.' The next day we took a loan out for twenty-five thousand dollars and gave it to Chad."

"You never saw Chad again."

"No. About a month later I never saw my husband again either. He just kind of faded away. Last I heard, he was in Minneapolis selling tires." She took a deep breath. "Unfortunately, my signature was on the loan. I'm still paying on it. I will be for years."

"I'm sorry."

"You live and learn, right?"

"Sometimes we do," I said softly.

Aria said, "Tell me about you."

I took a deep breath. "Me. I've lived in Daytona Beach for most of my life, except for a year at the University of North Florida in Jacksonville, where I mostly learned that college wasn't really for me. It was, for better or worse, where I met my wife. We were married for six years but divorced about a year ago."

"What happened?"

"I don't know. I mean, I thought I did. At first I thought it was because I traveled too much. And maybe that was it in the beginning, but in the end she had someone else."

"I'm sorry."

"Yeah. Me too. I wanted it to work."

"Do you have friends?"

"A few. My best friend is Nate. He works with me. But he's nothing like me."

"In what way?"

"He's tough. Like, Kevlar tough."

She asked, "Who's Kevlar?"

I smiled. "Sorry. Kevlar's what they make bulletproof vests from."

"Oh."

"This story explains him perfectly. Before Nate joined the marines he was delivering pizza. One night a guy walks up to him, pulls out a gun, and says, 'Give me all your money.' Nate looked at the gun, then at the guy, and said, 'Really? You brought a .38 to rob me? That's just going to make me mad.' And he turned and walked away. He said he kept waiting for the guy to shoot him in the back but he never did."

"He's tough or crazy?"

"Sometimes it's a fine line," I said.

She laughed. Then she yawned.

"You're tired," I said. "It's late."

"I'm sorry. I worked a double shift today. I was into work at five."

"Then I'd better get you home."

As we walked out the back of the diner we passed the Pino painting. Suddenly I stopped. "Wait a second."

"What?"

"Stand right here, next to this painting."

She looked at me like I was crazy but did as I asked.

"That's why," I said.

"That's why what?"

"Ever since I met you, I've been wondering why you looked so familiar. Look"—I motioned to the picture—"it looks just like you."

She looked at the painting for a moment. "I can kind of see that. And she's got the waitress thing going."

"Not *kind of*," I said. "She looks *exactly* like you. You could have modeled for the picture."

"I'm not as pretty as she is."

"Prettier," I said. "Even prettier." I glanced at her and she was looking at me gratefully. "All right," I said. "Let's get you home before you pass out from exhaustion."

I drove her back to the diner, pulling up next to her car behind the restaurant, an older-model Jeep Wrangler, covered with about a foot of snow.

She sighed when she saw it. "I'm buried."

"No worries," I said. "I just got this." I lifted my new snow brush-scraper. "I'm practically local. Just one minute." I left my car running as I brushed the snow off her Jeep, leaving huge mounds of snow on the ground around her car. After I finished I came back to my car and got in.

"Thank you," she said.

"My pleasure."

She smiled sweetly. "Pleasure? Really? You hate the cold." She took my wet, cold hands and looked at them. "Don't you have gloves?"

"I have cycling gloves," I said. "In Florida."

She began rubbing my hands. Then she lifted them to her mouth and blew on them with her warm breath. After a few times she said, "I think I've saved them."

"Thank you."

"Thank *you*. I had a really nice evening."

"Me too," I said. "Do you work tomorrow?"

"Yes. Another double."

"Then I'll see you tomorrow at dinner."

"I'd like that," she said. She looked at me a little nervously and then said, "Do you want to do something after work?"

"I would, but won't you be too tired?"

"I'm sure I will be," she said. "But, do you want to do something?"

"Yes. What would you like to do? Besides sleep."

She thought for a moment, then said, "I'll surprise you. Good night." She leaned over and kissed me on the cheek, then opened her door. She got out, stopped, and then turned back. "Do you know how long it's been since a man pulled out a chair for me or scraped the snow from my car?"

"No idea," I said.

"Yeah. Me neither." She closed the door and walked to her car. I waited for her to pull out before leaving myself. As I drove back to the inn, I realized that I was gradually losing interest in my hunt for LBH.

Chapter
Twenty-four

The next morning I hoped to see Ray at breakfast, but didn't. I wanted to talk to him about Aria. As I was about to leave the dining room, Lita walked through.

"Good morning, Mr. Bartlett. How is everything with your stay?"

"Everything's great," I said. "Where's Ray this morning?"

"He's visiting his grandchildren in Salt Lake. He'll be back tomorrow. Have a good day." She scurried off to help someone standing at the front counter.

I went up to my room and got ready for the day. I had at least three visits planned: Laurie Heger, Lisa Hewitt, and Louise Higham.

The first place I visited, the Laurie Heger residence, was an apartment about three miles east of the community center—a stretch, as far as festivalgoers walking by were concerned. Also, her window faced the opposite direction of the park. I couldn't imagine people walking by in crowds past her apartment during the festival. Americans don't walk that far. We just don't. If it's more than five minutes, we drive. Europeans will walk that far, but going to a Swiss festival doesn't make people Swiss.

I knocked, but no one answered. I crossed her off my list anyway.

My second stop was Lisa Hewitt. Unlike the previous prospect, Lisa lived only a half mile from the community center. There was a young woman in the driveway brushing snow off her car as I pulled up in front of the house. She watched me park, then, as I got out, she threw her brush inside her car and walked up to me. She looked to be in her late twenties. "Hi," she said brightly.

"Hi, I'm looking for Lisa Hewitt."

"That's me."

She seemed so forthright, I followed suit. "My name is Alex. I'm not from Midway. I'm just trying to find someone. She's a blogger from around here."

"Cool. What does she blog about?"

I had to think before I answered. I didn't want to say "loneliness," again revealing my aversion to the word. "Reflections on life, that sort of thing."

"Cool," she repeated. "How can I help?"

"I was wondering if it was you."

She laughed. "No way. I hate writing. In college it took me, like, an hour to write a paragraph for English."

"So you're not a blogger."

"No. I follow a few, though. Have you read Allie Brosh? She's hilarious."

"Is she the one with the funny, bizarre drawing of a fishlike thing?"

"Yeah, that's her! That's cool you know who she is." She took a step back, motioning to her running car. "Well, I better get to work. Good luck finding your bloggess." She turned and walked back to her car. I waved at her as she drove away.

That was easy, I thought. Another lead bites the list.

My next stop, Louise Higham, lived about four blocks northwest of the diner. Her house was run-down and in need of a paint job.

The doorbell had a piece of silver-gray duct tape across it, so I knocked. A moment later I heard steps, then an extremely large, middle-aged woman in a nightgown answered. She looked anxious.

"May I help you?"

"Hi. I'm looking for Louise Higham."

Awkwardly, she didn't say anything.

"Are you Louise?"

"No, sir. Louise lives in the apartment downstairs. It's around back."

I looked over to the side of the house to see if there was some kind of walkway. If there was one, it was covered in snow. "Is there a separate entrance?"

"Yes. It's over there. You'll have to open the gate."

"Do you know if she's home?"

She strained her head out the door to look at the carport. "That's her car there, so I suppose she is. No guarantee she'll answer."

"All right. Thank you."

"Please don't let the dog out."

She shut the door without saying good-bye. I walked around the side of the house to a tall wooden-plank fence and unlatched the gate. Immediately there was barking. I pushed open the gate just a few inches to look inside, mostly to see what kind of a dog it was. There was a medium-size, honey-colored collie standing on the covered back patio, her coat and belly white with snow. She continued barking but didn't leave the dry concrete.

The backyard was completely covered in snow. I put my shoulder against the gate to push it open just enough to squeeze through, then stepped into the snow. The dog was running around on the patio, barking like crazy.

"Come on, girl," I said, slightly stooping and putting out my arms. The dog came to me, her tail wagging as she bounded through the thick snow like a gazelle. She jumped up on me with snow-covered paws. I crouched down and scratched her for a while. After a few minutes, I stood, and the dog followed me over to the side of the house, where a vinyl awning jutted out over a concrete stairwell.

"Stay," I said. She obeyed.

I clutched the cold metal handrail and walked carefully down the icy stairs. If it weren't for the awning, the stairs would have looked like a mountain slope. It seemed like no one had been in or out of the place for a while. The landing was crowded with three full plastic garbage sacks, one partially opened, with trash—mostly beer cans and booze bottles—spilling out.

There was no doorbell, so I knocked on the door. It was a few minutes before the door opened to a red-faced, inebriated woman. She wore no makeup and her hair was matted to one side. Her blouse was unbuttoned, exposing her bra. The house stank like cats or some collection of animals.

"What do you want?" Her words were slurred.

"I'm looking for Louise Higham."

"What do you want?"

In her condition there was no reason not to speak plainly. "I'm looking for a blogger."

"A what?"

"A blogger." She just looked at me, so I added, "Someone who blogs."

"I don't dance."

There was really no need to explain. "Okay. Thank you."

She shut the door.

I petted the dog once more before leaving the yard, and I remembered to shut the gate.

Chapter
Twenty-five

After checking my list, I decided to go back to the Swiss home I had visited the day before—the one that was for sale.

This time there was a car parked out front. I walked in through the gate and was immediately greeted by a stout, redheaded woman. "Hello!"

"Are you Lindsey Harman?" I asked.

"No, Ms. Harman's already moved out. I'm Gloria, with Keller Williams Real Estate. Would you like to see the house?"

"No, I actually came to see Lindsey. I was interested in talking to her about her blog."

"I didn't know she had a blog."

"When do you expect her back?"

"I don't. She already moved to St. George with her boyfriend."

"Oh," I said, gleaning in one sentence all I needed to know about Lindsey Harman. "All right. Thanks for your help."

"Don't mention it. When I talk to her can I tell her anything?"

I turned back. "Sure. Just tell her to keep up the good work."

Just four names left. Actually, this wasn't really a good sign. Sometimes in my travels, while waiting at airport luggage carousels, I would guess how many bags it would take before mine appeared. What I learned is that if my bag didn't come before the last ten, chances were great that it wouldn't make it at all, and I'd have to go stand in the lost baggage line with all the other tormented people. What were the odds that LBH was among the last four leads? Or was fate just teasing me?

Even though I was near the Mistletoe Diner, I didn't want to wear out my welcome with Aria, so I drove past it two blocks to a local burger stand and got a chicken sandwich, fries, and Coke. When I got back to the inn I checked my phone messages. Satisfied that there wasn't anything that was going to cost me my job, I rolled over and fell asleep. Other than that haze of a month when Jill had left me, I don't remember ever taking so many naps in my life. Maybe it was the altitude. Or maybe I was just finally catching up on two-million-plus miles of travel.

I drove to the diner around seven. The parking lot wasn't particularly crowded but the restaurant was. Ridiculously crowded. Every table and booth was taken and there were at least two dozen people standing around the *Please Wait to Be Seated* sign.

Aria, who was bouncing from booth to table, didn't see me until she came to the front to seat the next guests. She smiled at me wearily. "I'm so sorry, we're slammed. If you don't mind, just take that seat at the counter."

"Thanks."

I started to walk when a man standing next to me said angrily, "Excuse me, Miss. We were here first."

Aria didn't flinch. "I'm sorry, he has reservations. Do you have reservations?"

The man just looked at her blankly.

"I'll be with you shortly."

"You've done that before," I said to her when we had taken a few steps.

"More than once."

I took the last seat at the counter. It was a few minutes before Aria got back to me. She brought me a plain lemonade. "I'm so sorry. This is crazy."

"What's going on?"

"There's a crèche convention going on at the community center. They came here on a bus, so they all walked here."

"What's a crèche convention?"

"They're for people who collect nativity scenes. You know, a crèche . . ."

I shrugged. I had never heard the word.

She took a deep breath. "Anyway, about tonight . . ."

My heart fell. Considering her circumstances, I figured she was going to cancel. I wouldn't blame her.

". . . I'll probably be a half hour later. Do you still want to go?"

"Of course. Are you sure you're up to it?"

"Absolutely."

"Excellent," I said. "I'll be here."

Not surprisingly, we didn't talk much, even though she smiled at me in passing. After I finished eating, I waved to her and she came up to me. She was out of breath. "How was everything?"

"Thelma's in good form."

"Thelma's always in good form." She took a deep breath. "So, I forgot to tell you something about tonight. Wear a swimsuit."

"We're going swimming?"

"Sort of. And wear a robe or something or you'll freeze." She smiled. "See you at eleven thirty."

Wear a robe?

Instead of going directly back to my room, I decided to explore a little and drove east to downtown Heber. The town of Heber is larger than Midway and a four-lane highway runs through the center of it. Both sides of the road are crowded with businesses and restaurants.

In addition to the commercial section's decorations and light-strewn trees, the street was decorated for the season with large strands of tinsel crisscrossing the road at intersections. Oversize lighted plastic candy canes were fastened to the streetlamps that lined the highway. It pleased me to see it. Christmas Americana.

I stopped in a grocery store to buy some

sundries—deodorant, shaving cream, and razors —then drove back to the inn.

At a quarter past eleven I put on my swimsuit, donned the thick terry-cloth robe from the inn, and put my shoes back on. I thought of wearing my parka over the robe but decided I'd rather die of exposure than look that stupid. I walked downstairs and handed my key to Claudia at the front desk. "I'll be back in a couple hours."

"You're going out in a robe?"

"I'll bring it back," I said.

"That wasn't my concern," she said, raising her eyebrows. "It's subfreezing. Keep warm."

"No guarantees," I said. I pushed open the door and the brisk, chill air hit me in the face like a slap. I walked out to my car and got inside. I could feel the cold of the vinyl seat through my robe. *It's freaking Antarctica,* I thought. My windshield was frosted inside and out so I started the car, turned on the front and rear defrosters, and sat for nearly ten minutes while the heater cleared up the windshields. Once I could see, I drove to the diner.

I arrived to see Aria's white Jeep idling at the far end of the parking lot, evidenced by a cloud of smoke and steam billowing out of its tail- pipe. As I pulled in next to her, Aria stepped out of her car. She didn't have a robe but wore a long peacoat with her bare legs exposed at the bottom. On her otherwise bare feet, she was wearing only flip-flops.

"Aren't you cold?" I asked, climbing out of my car.

"Freezing," she said, smiling. "The trick is not minding the pain."

I grinned. "Sorry I'm late. My windshield was frozen."

"No worries," she said. "Nice robe."

"Thanks. It's from the inn."

"I know. It has a pig head on it."

"So, couldn't we have just changed into our suits wherever we're going?"

She cocked her head. "We could have, but I don't know you that well. Come on, get in. I'll drive."

I climbed into the passenger seat of her Jeep. I noticed that the back side window was broken and covered with a black plastic garbage sack duct-taped to the window frame. The heater was blowing loudly in compensation.

"Sorry, my car's a mess. I haven't had time to clean it."

"How did your window break?" I asked.

"Some kids threw a snowball at it."

"Recently?"

"Last year."

She pulled out onto Main Street, which, not surprisingly, was deserted. We drove about a half mile west, then pulled off onto a dark side road still partially covered with snow. The road looked like it led up into the mountains and I couldn't see any sign of a building or any place to swim.

We continued past a grove of bare trees that opened into a large, snow-covered meadow. "In the summer this is all covered with sunflowers," she said. "It's beautiful. I love sunflowers."

"Me too," I said. What actually came to mind was the time I gave Jill a bouquet of sunflowers for her twenty-eighth birthday. She asked me why I had given her weeds.

"Just down this road is where we used to cut our Christmas trees," Aria said.

"You can cut your own?"

"Yes. You need a permit, but it's easy to get, and the trees are just right here."

"I've always wanted to do that," I said.

"Then why don't you?"

"There's not a lot of Christmas trees in Daytona Beach."

"No, but at least you could find a starfish for the star on top."

About two hundred yards from where we had turned off we came to another grove of trees. Aria pulled to the side of the road and turned off the Jeep. It sputtered once like a mechanical death-rattle, then died. "We're here."

I looked around at the snow-covered landscape. The crystalline white sea of snow reflected a bright moon. "Where are we?"

"The hot pot," she said. She grabbed a towel from the backseat, opened her door, and stepped out. A moment later I followed, stepping out onto the tundra-like road. The cold air bit my exposed legs, and the only noise I could hear was the Jeep's hot engine ticking and Aria's footsteps as she crunched through the crusted snow in her flip-flops. The snow came nearly to the bottom of her coat.

She was walking toward a mound about sixty steps from the Jeep. At the top, there was a crater where the snow was melted, revealing porous-looking lumps of rocks. Heat rose from the hot water, turning to steam in the cold air, almost as thick as smoke from a bonfire.

The hot spring was surrounded by a wire fence excessively posted with *No Trespassing* signs, something I was keenly aware of after my visit to the crazy Mace woman.

Aria twisted the wire off the fence and pulled it back as if she had done it a hundred times before.

I looked around. "Is this legal?"

"That depends on what you mean by *legal,*" she said.

"Will someone arrest us?"

"No. It's a small town."

I nodded. "Okay, no problem."

"The owner might shoot us for trespassing. But you like taking risks, don't you?" She stepped inside the wire cage, set down the towel, then took off her coat, folding it carefully over a rock. She was wearing a black bikini that showed off her beautifully curved body. She covered up well in her work smock, because honestly, she was even more beautiful than I had noticed or imagined.

I think she must have noticed my attention and she smiled. "Well? Are you coming? Or are you afraid of . . . *trespassing?*"

The way she looked, I would have eaten my way through the fence, No Trespassing signs and all. "I'm coming."

I followed her over the rocks. The top of the hot pot had the rough, layered texture of an oyster's shell. As I neared the rim, Aria took off her flip-flops and carefully picked her way down the rock to a small outcropping that jutted out about three feet below the rim. She smiled at me, then stepped off into the water. She came up with a loud sigh. "Come in. It feels so good."

I looked down into the steaming crater. The dark pool looked bottomless and had an acrid sulfur smell. "I'll be right there."

I took off my robe and lay it over a rock next to Aria's coat. Then, sitting on my robe, I removed my shoes and put them next to her flip-flops. I walked over to the crater's rim.

"Is this where you get in?"

"Uh-huh."

As I started lowering myself down the ledge I slipped, throwing myself into the middle of the pot. I came up, sputtering.

"Nice entrance," she said, her voice slightly echoing in the cavernous rock. "You didn't have to do that to impress me."

"As long as you're impressed."

The water was hot but not uncomfortable. I swam over to her. She was holding on to a narrow ledge of rock. Six feet off to her side was a homemade rope ladder. It must have been there for a while, as it was white with mineral deposits.

"This is so healing for your body," she said. "It's perfect after a long day on your feet."

"What kind of rock is this?"

"Limestone. This crater was formed by the minerals in this water. Actually, it has a name. Tufa. I remember that because it reminds me of tofu. The name, not its taste."

"It probably tastes better than tofu," I said, adding, "I hate tofu." I swam over to the ladder and rested on it. "So, do many people know about this place?"

"Locals. But they don't come here."

"Because they'll get shot?"

She smiled. "Maybe." After a moment she said, "Actually, the man who owns this land is a customer of mine. I serve him ham and runny eggs on wheat toast every morning. He told me that I can come up here anytime."

"So the shooting part . . ."

"I was just teasing."

"Teasing or testing?"

"Pick one." She swam over next to me. "Still cold?"

"No. How hot is the water?"

"Most of the hot pots in Midway are considered warm springs instead of hot springs. This one is ninety-eight degrees, a little below body temperature." She floated closer to me. "Turn around."

"How come?"

"You ask too many questions. Trust me."

"All right." I turned away from her.

"Now hold on to the ladder."

I clutched the ladder and leaned into it, my forehead resting on one of the rungs. Aria put her hand on the back of my neck and began to rub it. The water had a slick, gel-like consistency that made her hand glide easily over my flesh.

"How does that feel?"

I softly groaned with pleasure.

"So you like it."

"Yes, ma'am."

"I'm not a ma'am."

After another minute of her massage I turned back and looked into her eyes.

"I don't know what we're doing, but I haven't been this happy for a very long time."

"Me too," she said.

"And I think you just might be the most beautiful woman in the world."

She smiled. "I think you're beautiful too." She moved in a little closer, her eyes locked on mine. "Very."

"I have a question about your job," I said.

"That's what you're thinking about right now?"

"It's relevant. Do your customers always try to kiss you under the mistletoe?"

"How is that relevant?"

"You ask too many questions," I said.

Her smile widened a little, then she said, "Only the wrong customers."

"What would happen if I tried?"

"I don't know. Why don't you find out?"

For a moment we just looked into each other's eyes. Then I began to lean forward. She leaned forward too, until our lips met, lightly at first, then exploding into full passion.

I had one arm hooked through the ladder and reached out with the other and put it around her narrow waist, pulling her into me. She put both arms around me. The softness of her body and lips was the most exquisite thing I'd felt for a very long time.

I don't know how long we'd been kissing when someone shouted, "What are you doing in there?"

We looked up to see an old man in a fringed leather rancher jacket and a cowboy hat standing above the rim of the crater. He was holding a shotgun.

Aria swam out away from me toward the center of the pool. "Cal, it's me. Aria."

The man bent down a little and squinted. "Aria?"

"Yes, it's me."

He still didn't look happy. He lowered his gun.

"Sorry. Didn't know it was you. Earl Belnap called and said I had some hippies in my pot."

Hippies in his pot?

He looked at me and his eyes flashed. "Who's the boy?"

"This is Alex. He's a friend of mine."

"Nice to meet you, sir," I said.

He ignored me. "Sure you don't need me to shoot him?"

I couldn't tell if he was serious. He might have been. Aria stifled a laugh. "No. Not this time. I'll let you know if that changes."

"All right," he said still looking a bit miffed. "Don't drown or nothin'."

"Thanks, Cal. Love you."

"Yeah," he drawled. He slowly picked his way back down the crater, mumbling and swinging his shotgun like a baton.

Aria turned back to me. "You thought you were going to get shot, didn't you?"

"Maybe."

"So, was it worth it?"

"Was what worth it?"

"Getting shot just to kiss me."

I reached out for her. "Definitely."

A large smile crossed her face and she swam back to me, pushing her body up against mine. "Where were we?"

I put my arms back around her and we went back to kissing.

Chapter
Twenty-six

After a half hour she said, "We can go back to my place."

"You're not too tired?"

"I think I just got my second wind."

We got out of the spring, the water on our bodies steaming in the freezing air. Fortunately, Aria had guessed that I would not think of bringing a towel and had brought two. She handed me one, and I quickly dried off and put on my robe. We slipped our shoes back on, then walked down to her Jeep.

"You drive," she said.

"Where am I going?"

"I'll show you," she said. "Just go back toward the diner."

I did a three-point turnaround and headed back to town, following Aria's directions about a quarter mile past the diner to a small duplex just behind a gas station on Main.

"This is where you live?"

"Uh-huh. Cheap rent."

"You're close to the diner."

"Yes. I usually just walk to work, unless it's icy or I'm working late." She unlocked the door and we went inside. The apartment was simple but tidy, with a few chairs and a simple black sofa behind a rectangular wooden coffee table. On one side of the room, next to the wall, was a computer table with an older-model PC.

There was a framed quote on the wall.

NOT ALL THOSE WHO WANDER ARE LOST.

"I like that," I said.

"I thought of getting a tattoo of it," Aria replied.

"Why didn't you?"

She smiled. "I didn't want a tattoo." She walked out of the room, returning a minute later wearing sweats. "Would you like some herbal tea?"

"Yes, please."

"I have peppermint and chamomile."

"Chamomile will put me to sleep."

"Peppermint it is."

She boiled water in a kettle, then brought two cups out to the coffee table. After she sat I tried the tea, then said, "I have a question. I hope it's not too personal."

"Yes?"

"After Wade left, why didn't you go back to Minnesota?"

She looked down for a moment, then said, "It wasn't much of an option."

"Why is that?"

"My mother's there." I could see the emotion this confession brought.

"You don't get along with your mother?"

"No." She took a sip of her tea, then set down her cup. "My mother was emotionally ill. She had been diagnosed as schizophrenic, but she wouldn't get help and she wouldn't take her medications.

"When I was seven she started telling everyone that my father was sexually abusing me—my schoolteachers, the neighbors, our pastor. Eventually the police came and arrested him.

"My mother was always telling me that men were bad. She made me tell the police that my father was abusing me, even though he wasn't." She shook her head. "She was sick. My father was a good man. Even with what she did, he tried to help her. He tried to protect me from her.

"Then she filed for divorce and a restraining order. I don't know how she got the restraining order. The laws in this country are against fathers. They assume they're guilty until proven innocent. But it was my testimony . . ." She teared up. "I betrayed the one person who was protecting me."

The thought that she had falsely accused him made me sick, but it wasn't her fault. It was her mother's. "You weren't old enough to know better."

She wiped a tear from her cheek. "He wasn't found guilty. But he left. After that my mother only got worse. She didn't have him to torment, so she turned her crazy elsewhere.

"She believed that the government was spying on us. She told me that any red lights in the house meant that the CIA, the FBI, and a secret organization she couldn't reveal were tracking our movements. Every night we would have to go around the house in the dark and unplug everything with a light—the microwave, clocks, everything. She said that they could shoot lasers through the lights that would control our minds.

"She had also read that the government had added chemicals to jet fuel so the tracks you see in the sky behind jets was really poison flying down on us to brainwash us."

"When did you begin to see through it?"

"My first boyfriend helped me. I was fourteen, he was seventeen. He would laugh when I'd tell him things my mother said. He wasn't the first person to tell me my mother was crazy, but he was the first I believed.

"Then something happened that really opened my eyes. At the time I was doing all of the cooking. One evening after dinner I heard her on the phone calling poison control. She told them that she had been poisoned.

"Then she ran to the store and bought these charcoal pills and started swallowing them. She must have taken too many of them because she started throwing up all over until she passed out. I called 911. The paramedics came, and they rushed her to emergency.

"When she came to, she told the doctors that I had poisoned her. The doctors knew she wasn't well. They had a psychiatrist visit her. Afterward he took me aside and told me that my mother was schizophrenic and a borderline personality." She took a deep breath. "The thing is, when crazy is normal, normal is crazy. I had to rebuild my entire world."

"Do you have siblings?"

"No. I was an only child, thank God. She would have messed them up too. What I had was a string of boyfriends. But my mother's crazy seeped into that as well. In a way, I was trying to match the paradigm my mother had programmed into me that men were bad, so I looked for bad men, the wild, mean ones. I think, in some wacked-out way, I was still trying to make my mother's crazy right so I could make sense of the world." She looked at me. "You think I'm crazy now, don't you?"

"No. I think you're resilient."

"Thank you," she said. "So I moved in with Wade when I was sixteen and we got married the day I turned eighteen. We were married on my birthday. Six months later, his cousin offered him a job in Midway, Utah, and here I am."

"Here you are," I said.

"And here you are," she said, touching my arm. She took a deep breath. "Yesterday you asked me why I was waiting outside at the diner."

"Yes."

"Wade and I lived a few miles north of here. We only had one car, so he would drive me to and from work. He used to get raging mad at me if I wasn't outside waiting for him after my shift. Sometimes he'd be almost an hour late picking me up. I'd be nearly frozen." She slowly shook her head. "He was an angry man."

"I'm sorry," I said.

"I'm glad he left town."

I squeezed her hand. "How about your father now? Do you ever talk to him?"

She looked down for a moment. "Almost every day." When she looked back up her eyes were moist. She said, "So I've told you all my secrets. Now you need to tell me one."

"What would you like to know?"

"I'd like to know, Mr. Bartlett, what you are really doing in Midway."

"You don't believe that I'm here for work?"

She slowly shook her head. "No, we have two traffic signals. We don't need software for that."

"I should have known you were smarter than that."

"The truth is, I was willing to give you the benefit of the doubt, except I've had two customers tell me that there's a stranger in town who looks just like you, making random visits to women."

"Wow."

"Like I've said, it's a very small town."

"Fair enough. But now I'm the one who's going to sound crazy. I hope you're still willing to give me the benefit of the doubt."

"Try me."

I clasped my hands together. "Here goes. I came here to find someone."

"You're a bounty hunter?"

I grinned. "No. It's someone I met on the Internet. Actually, that's not quite true. We've never actually met." I looked up into her eyes. "This is going to sound really crazy. I mean, it's the craziest thing I've ever done."

"I know crazy," she said.

"This person, this woman, she wrote a blog that really spoke to me."

"What kind of blog?"

"She writes about loneliness and love. It was so honest and vulnerable . . . after all the lies in my marriage, to hear someone speak so honestly . . . I decided I had to meet her. But she didn't leave any information on her website except her initials."

"You came all the way to Midway to find someone with only their initials?"

"I know, crazy, right? I mean, if it was New York, I wouldn't have tried. But, like you said, Midway's a small town."

"What are her initials?"

"LBH."

Aria was quiet for a moment. I could see her thinking.

"Do you know anyone with those initials?" I asked.

She shook her head. "No. Mrs. Harding. But she's eighty years old."

"Yeah, I found that out."

"She's one of the customers who told me about you."

"She could talk like no one I've ever met," I said.

Aria smiled. "She's lonely. And she's very sweet. She's the only one who comes into the diner and brings us food." She looked into my eyes. "So how do you even know this LBH is in Midway?"

"For a long time I didn't. Then, in one of her blog entries she wrote about Swiss Days. I looked up Swiss Days on the Internet and Midway, Utah, was the only place that celebrated it at the time she wrote about. So I came out to see if I could find her."

"And when you find her, what will you do?"

"I don't know." I took her hand. "Things aren't the way I thought they'd be. I didn't plan on meeting you."

She smiled coyly. "That wasn't in my script either. So, will you keep on looking?"

"I don't know. Part of me feels like I need closure with this woman."

"And the other part of you?"

I leaned into her and we kissed.

We talked and kissed until Aria couldn't keep her eyes open and asked what time it was. "Almost three," I whispered.

She lightly groaned. "I have to be at work in three hours."

"I'm sorry," I said.

She smiled dreamily. "I'm not." I kissed her good night.

"I better let you sleep tomorrow," I said.

"I don't want to sleep."

"You need sleep. Do you work on Saturday?"

"No."

"Good. We'll go cut down a Christmas tree," I said.

"Why would I want to cut down a Christmas tree?"

"Because it's almost Christmas. And I may never get another chance."

"Whatever you say," she said. "As long as I get to be with you."

I got back to the inn about half past three. In spite of the hour, I didn't fall right to sleep. I didn't want to sleep. I wanted to relive the night in my memory. I just wanted to be with her. So why did I feel like I needed to keep looking for LBH?

Chapter
Twenty-seven

I didn't wake the next morning until after ten. I pulled on the same clothes I'd worn the day before and walked down to the dining room. I sat in my usual place and ordered griddle cakes with a side of sausage.

I was almost done eating when Ray walked into the room. In spite of the cold he was wearing long shorts with knee-high socks and thick leather walking boots. He looked very German. He also had a brown leather satchel slung over his arm.

He smiled when he saw me. "Mr. Bartlett," he said. "Just the man I'm looking for." He walked over and sat down at my table. He shrugged off the satchel, put it on the table next to him, then looked into my eyes. "I'm glad you are here, my friend. I need to talk to you."

He leaned closer and, in a more serious tone, said, "You know, the longer I live, the more I believe in heaven ordinant—the Shakespearean edict that 'there's a divinity that shapes our ends, rough-hew them how we will.' " He leaned back and his voice relaxed. "So, did you find your LBH?"

I wiped my mouth with my napkin. "Not yet."

I was about to tell him that I was considering aborting my search when he said, "I didn't think so. Let me tell you why. I have a story to tell you.

"Nine years ago I was at an art showing in Park City when a man asked me for some help. He was trying to get his elderly grandmother in a wheelchair down a set of stairs. I don't know where the ramp was, but the stairs only had five steps, so I offered my assistance.

"We're just about down the last step when *pop!* something gives in my back. I ruptured a disk, L5-S1. It pinched off my sciatic nerve, so I've got no feeling in my left leg. Hurt like the devil. Two surgeries and a diskectomy later, I can walk without a cane. It's like they say, 'no good deed goes unpunished.' " He leaned forward until he was uncomfortably close. "You're probably wondering why I'm sharing this story."

"It crossed my mind," I said.

"My back's been sore ever since. So once a month I treat myself to a massage. There's a wonderful, beautiful young lady in Midway with nothing short of magical hands. So the day before yesterday I was getting my monthly massage when it occurred to me that this young lady is not on your list, but she should be.

"Her name is Lynette Hurt. Granted, it's a bit of an unfortunate name for that profession, or maybe it's ideal, I don't know. She lives in Heber, which is why you didn't have her on your list, but her parlor, or studio, whatever they call them these days, is only a few blocks from the park. She gets a lot of business during Swiss Days."

"How old is she?"

"About your age. Maybe a few years younger."

"And she's single?"

"She's been single and alone for a while now. Her husband was killed in a tractor accident just on the other side of the Homestead. What a tragic day that was for the community."

"And her family?"

"She never had any children and his family moved away after their son's death, so she's very much alone. And lonely. She told me. I don't know if she blogs, but I know she's very active on the social media, Facebook and such." He pointed a sausage finger at me. "I think Lynette's your woman. She's a sweet one. Lonely. Contemplative. Pretty, in a natural way, you know, not one to wear a lot of makeup. Doesn't need it. Soft eyes. Soft-spoken . . ."

"Does she have a middle name?"

"I honestly don't know. But I do know that her maiden name was German. Bucher. It means beech tree or something like that."

"Her father was German," I said. "LBH mentioned that in one of her posts."

Ray nodded. "Yes, Lynette Bucher Hurt."

I looked at him. "Her initials are LBH."

"Yes, sir." He reached over and patted me on the shoulder. "I knew that wouldn't be lost on you. I'll have Claudia schedule you an appointment for her next available opening."

"Thank you," I said.

He then took something from his satchel. "Here, I brought something for you." He handed me a small cluster of dried flowers bundled together with twine. "It's edelweiss. It's an important symbol to the Swiss. Edelweiss grows high in the mountains on rocky soil, so if a young man wanted to impress a young lady, he would bring her edelweiss. She might not marry him, but it would certainly get her attention. I thought it might come in handy."

"It's very strange that you would bring this to me." I looked him in the eyes. "In one of the blog entries LBH wrote that her father told her to wait for a man to bring her edelweiss."

Ray smiled. "There you go. Just as I was saying. Divinity."

My breakfast with Ray had left me feeling a little confused. *Had I really found LBH?* I realized that there was a part of me that had actually doubted that I would ever find her. And, in consequence of my budding relationship with Aria, there was now a part of me that didn't want to find her.

Still, I had to see this through. I had to know. The fact that the woman was a masseuse was convenient. I could casually talk to her about her life without creeping her out or making her suspicious. I don't know if it was divinity, as Ray claimed, but it couldn't have worked out better.

After breakfast I went back up to get ready for the day. I was shaving when my room phone rang. I wiped the shaving cream off my face and answered.

"Mr. Bartlett, it's Claudia at the front desk. I just wanted to let you know that I was able to get you a one-hour massage appointment with Ms. Hurt at two o'clock this afternoon."

"Thank you."

As I hung up the phone, I realized that after all the miles and all I'd been through, I might actually be meeting LBH. So why was it that I couldn't stop thinking of Aria?

Chapter
Twenty-eight

Before I left the inn, Claudia handed me the address of the massage studio. It was just three doors north of Main Street, in a small, single-story house. I passed the diner on the way there and I couldn't help but look for Aria. I didn't see her. I parked in the street, then walked up to the front door. A plastic sign read:

Awaken Massage by Lynette
Swedish • Shiatsu • Hot Stone •
Deep Tissue • Reflexology
9 a.m.–6 p.m. / Mon–Fri / Walk-ins welcome

I stepped inside. The home's front room had been converted into a lounge area with a modern, bright red sofa behind a glass coffee table covered with magazines on massage therapy, health, and holistic healing. The space had a comforting ambience.

I examined the room carefully, looking for clues. On a counter in the corner of the room was a scented candle whose fragrance filled the room with a pleasant pineapple-citrus smell. Next to the counter was a cabinet with a glass front. I walked over to inspect what was inside. There were small, amber apothecary bottles filled with different types of essential oils: lavender, frankin-cense, lemon, and at least a dozen others.

I sat down on the couch to wait. My anticipation was growing, teased by a sign hanging from the door in front of me:

Massage in Progress
Please be quiet,
I will be right with you.
—LBH

There it was. LBH. I checked my watch. I was early for my appointment. I had just started reading an article on the benefits of cupping therapy when the hallway door opened. I looked up to see an attractive young woman with short blond hair step out. She had wide, fleshy cheeks and soft blue eyes. Even though her maiden name was German, I thought she was more Swedish-looking. She was wearing a short-sleeved, dark blue smock.

There was something very surreal about finally seeing her.

"Mr. Bartlett?"

I stood. "Yes."

She smiled. "No, please, sit. My client is getting dressed. She's elderly, so it takes her a little longer. I'll be right back to get you. Please relax and make yourself comfortable."

"Thank you," I said.

She disappeared back through the door. About five minutes later an older woman came walking out from the hallway. She was a little bent, with silver hair that was slightly mussed from her massage. She was speaking to Lynette. "I'll be out of town next week, and it's the holiday, so I won't need my usual appointment. But I'll be back the next."

"Where are you going?"

"Up north," she said. "Logan. McKenzie—that's Barry's second daughter—is marrying one of those Logan boys. On Christmas Eve, no less. I don't know what she's thinking."

Lynette walked out behind her, smiling. "Well, travel safe. And don't forget to do your stretches. Fifteen minutes a night."

"You sound just like my daughter. She keeps trying to get me to go to one of those yoga classes."

"You should try it. I've seen it do wonders."

The old woman rooted through her purse for a moment, lifted out a hundred-dollar bill, and handed it to Lynette. "Thank you, dear. It's the best hour of my week. And keep the extra. Christmas is coming."

"You don't need to do that."

"You deserve it. Have a merry Christmas."

The women hugged and the elderly woman left, furtively glancing at me. There was a brief pause, as if in deference to the woman's departure, then Lynette walked up to me, extending her hand.

"Hi, I'm Lynette."

I stood and took her hand. "I'm Alex."

"Thank you for your patience, Alex. Come on back."

As I followed her I said, "Thank you for getting me in on such short notice."

"You're welcome. I always try to accommodate the local resorts. They're my bread and butter."

She led me to an open door at the end of the corridor. Inside the room was a wide massage table covered with beige cotton sheets. The room was dimmed and light, Asian-sounding flute music was playing against a background ambience of nature sounds.

"Go ahead and get undressed to your comfort level, then slide under the sheet with your face down. I'll go wash my hands and I'll be right back."

She shut the door. I took off all my clothes, folded them in the corner, then climbed onto the warm table, pulling the sheet over my back. I rested my head in the cradle. I wondered if Lynette's hands would feel as good as Aria's. My thoughts were interrupted by a light knock on the door.

"May I come in?"

"Yes."

I could hear the door open as she stepped inside. She dimmed the lights a little more, shut the door, and walked over next to me, gently putting her hand on the middle of my back. "Have you had a massage before?"

"Many."

"Good. Do you have a preference today? Deep tissue, relaxation, hot stones . . ."

"Just relaxation," I said.

"Are there any places you would like me to pay special attention?"

My heart. "My scalp," I said. "And my feet."

"Whatever you like." She poured oil onto her hands, rubbed them together, and then lightly pulled the sheet down to my lower back. "Just let me know if the pressure is too much." She ran her hand up my spine and began rubbing the oil into my back. Her hands were soft yet strong.

She had worked my back for a few minutes when I asked, "Have you been doing this long?"

"Almost six years," she said. "You're staying at the Blue Boar?"

"Yes."

"It's a beautiful inn. Have you stayed there before?"

"No. This is my first time in Midway. Actually, in Utah."

"What do you think of it?"

"I think it's cold."

She laughed. "Where are you from, California?"

"Florida."

"The other side." She pressed on a tender spot beneath my right shoulder blade and I recoiled a little. "Sorry, you've got a knot here. Let me work it out."

Neither of us spoke as she rubbed the area.

"Do you have a lot of stress in your life?"

"The usual," I said.

She kept rubbing until the tension was gone.

"You're good," I said. "Do you get a lot of business here?"

"I keep busy. I do a lot of work for the resorts, Zermatt and the Homestead. In the fall there's a festival here called Swiss Days. I'm pretty much nonstop those days and for several weeks after.

"There's a parking lot on the other side of this block, so there's constant traffic and I get a lot of walk-ins. Sometimes I wonder where all those people come from."

I recognized those words from her blog.

"There's also a lot of new development going on around here. It's not Park City with the celebrities and all that, but there's still a lot of new money coming into the city. It makes the locals kind of crazy, these new people moving in with their own ideas. Some of these families have been here since the Mormon pioneers."

"How long have you lived here?"

"I moved here eight years ago, but my husband's family goes way back to the pioneers." She paused. "Take a deep breath, then slowly breathe out."

I did as she said.

"What brings you to Midway?"

I hesitated. "Business."

"What kind of business are you in?"

"I'm an assassin."

She was quiet for a moment, then said, "Do you get health benefits with that?"

We both laughed. I liked this woman.

After a half hour Lynette had me roll over onto my back. I looked into her face and she smiled. She had a kind smile. I could imagine her writing the kinds of blog entries that had brought me three thousand miles west.

"Do you do much on the Internet?" I asked.

"I try. I have a Facebook page and an Instagram account. Nothing big, a few hundred people, but for a town this size, that's not bad. I also have a blog, but that's just for personal things."

"I'd like to read it."

She looked uncomfortable. "It's kind of embarrassing. It's just my thoughts. I write for self-therapy. I'd hate to actually meet someone who read it." She took a deep breath. "How do you feel?"

"I feel great," I said. "You have a very nice touch."

"Thank you."

I closed my eyes and let her finish her work in silence. I'd found LBH. Now what?

Chapter
Twenty-nine

As Lynette worked my scalp, I thought over my next move. I was confused. This is what I'd come three thousand miles for. I should have been wildly excited, not wildly conflicted. LBH was exactly what I hoped she'd be: kind, sincere, beautiful. But my heart was somewhere else. It was like going to a car dealership to purchase the car you've done all the research on and then your head gets turned by a model you've never even heard of. I don't mean to sound that shallow, comparing these women to cars, but you get my point.

Still, as I'd told Nate, I had felt powerfully inspired to find LBH, and now I had. I supposed that I owed it to the universe at least to see where it went from here.

Twenty minutes later Lynette ran her hands\ down the length of my body then gently set a hand on my knee. "That's our session, Alex. How do you feel?"

"Like a new man," I said.

"Good. I'm going to step out so you can dress. Would you like some water?"

"Please."

"I'll be right outside the door," she said. After she left the room, I just lay there in the darkness, taking deep breaths. The next move was mine. I sat up and dressed, then walked out into the hallway. Lynette was standing near the door, holding a plastic cup of water. "There you go," she said, handing me the cup.

I took a drink. "Thank you."

"Remember to drink a lot of water. There was a lot of tension built up in your neck and shoulders that I worked out, and you want to flush the toxins out of your system."

I followed her out to the lobby. I was glad that there was no one waiting. I gave her a credit card and signed on an extra twenty-dollar tip.

"Do you leave town soon?" she asked.

"Next week," I said. "I was going to leave on the twenty-second, but I might stay a little longer."

She grinned. "More people to kill?"

"So many hits, so little time."

"Well, if you ever come back into town, be sure to stop by. Unless you're coming on business. Then I've moved."

I laughed.

She grabbed a business card. "Here. In case you find yourself back in Midway."

I looked over the card, which basically had the same information as the front door, with the addition of her cell phone number. I realized that our time was at an end and I needed to act now.

"I don't know if this is appropriate or not, it's

kind of spontaneous, but would you like to go to dinner with me tonight?"

She looked as surprised at my invitation as I was. "I've never gone out with a client . . ."

"There's a first time for everything, right?"

She thought for a moment then smiled. "Yes. I'd like that. What time?"

"What's good for you?"

She looked at the clock on the wall. "It's almost two-thirty. I need to get a few things done at home. Say seven?"

"Seven would be great. I don't know a lot of restaurants in town, but the one at the Blue Boar is nice."

"The Blue Boar is very nice. Shall I meet you there?"

"Or I can pick you up," I said. "If you're okay with that."

"Thank you. Let me write my home address on the card."

I handed her the card and she scrawled something on the back and returned it to me. "Thank you. I'll see you at seven."

Sometime during my massage it had started snowing again. I brushed off my car, then headed back to the inn. As I drove down Main Street, I glanced at the diner. This time I thought I saw Aria inside and it made my stomach ache a little. I wanted to see her.

. . .

When I got to my room I called Nate and then Dale, but neither answered. I checked my emails, then pulled up LBH's blog. Not surprisingly, there was nothing new. One by one I reread her previous posts. They felt different now that I could put a face to them.

At six-thirty I went downstairs. The dining room was the most crowded I'd seen it since I'd arrived. I'd gotten used to just walking in at my convenience and forgotten that the restaurant was open to the public and I might need reservations, especially on a Friday night a week before Christmas. Claudia was still at the front desk.

"How was your massage?" she asked.

"Perfect. In fact, I'm taking Lynette to dinner tonight."

She smiled. "That did go well."

"I was planning on bringing her here for dinner, but it looks like you're already full. Do you have any openings?"

"We always have openings for our inn guests," she said. "There's a private party here tonight, but we can seat you in Truffle Hollow, if that's okay."

"That would be fine. Thank you."

Lynette lived on the north side of Midway in an older, fairly large home, a long, white, stucco-

259

walled rambler. The street in front of her home was lined with trees, and as I pulled into her driveway I could see a horse stall and corral in her backyard. There was also a picturesque red barn about fifty yards behind the house. The home was decorated for the holidays with colorful lights outlining its frame. There was also a large, snow-shrouded plastic Nativity scene in the center of the yard. The bulbs of the four electric porch lights had been replaced with red and green bulbs for the season.

I rang the doorbell and Lynette promptly answered. She was wearing a form-fitting burgundy sequin dress with a wide gold belt that accentuated the narrow curvature of her waist. She looked stunning.

"Hi, come in," she said.

"Thank you." I stepped inside. The front room was also decorated for the season. There was an upright piano in the center of the room with plaster figurines of Christmas carolers arranged on the top. The fireplace had pink angel hair stretched along its mantel. Above the fireplace was a Thomas Kinkade print of a snow-covered gazebo next to an icy pond.

To the right of the fireplace was a tall, white-frosted Christmas tree hung with metallic blue baubles and white lights.

"Did you have any trouble finding me?" Lynette asked.

I almost burst out laughing. In light of what I'd been through in the last week, the question was funny. "Not at all," I said.

"Good. I'll just get my coat."

She returned wearing a full-length black wool coat that fell to her ankles.

"You look very nice," I said.

"I was thinking the same thing about you."

I opened the car door for her. As I climbed in she said, "This is a rental?"

"Yes."

"Is it good in the snow?"

"It's good, I'm not."

She smiled. "I'm excited about dinner. It's been at least two years since I've eaten at the Blue Boar."

"When I came down from my room tonight I was afraid that we might not be able to get a table because there was a private party. But since I'm a guest, they won't refuse me."

"You're telling me that you have friends in high places?"

"I think you're the one with friends in high places. One call from you to Ray and he would have served us dinner himself."

"He's a sweet guy."

"He is. But, just so you know, he hates it when pretty women call him that."

The restaurant was crowded but we had the pub to ourselves. For an appetizer I ordered the fondue for two, followed by the French onion gratinée and the filet mignon with crab-and-spinach-stuffed portobello and béarnaise sauce. Lynette ordered the Blue Boar salad and the duck breast with sour cherry purée.

After we'd been served our entrées I said, "I hope this isn't inappropriate, but Ray told me your husband passed away."

She nodded. "About seven years ago."

"I'm sorry."

"Thank you."

"So, tell me about yourself."

She wiped her mouth with a napkin. "I don't know the last time someone said that to me. In a small town, it's like everyone already knows everything about you. Or thinks they do." She shook her head. "I'm the pretty young widow, you know. The one every wife pities and fears."

"Fears?"

"I've actually seen them grab their husbands as I passed them on the sidewalk."

"I'm sorry. It's been seven years?"

"Seven long years." She sighed. "You know, you think you know what your life's going to look like, so you make these big plans, thinking you have some right to expect them. But it's like writing in the sand on the beach. The waves come up onto the shore and erase them and you're back to where you started."

I loved the poetry of her explanation. It reminded me of her blog posts.

"What about you? Have you ever been married?"

"Yes. But I'm divorced." I looked at her. "I hate saying that. It's like announcing failure. I never thought I'd be divorced. It just wasn't in my game plan."

"Did your parents divorce?"

"No, they stayed together. For better or worse. Mostly worse. They probably should have divorced."

"What happened with your marriage?"

"I thought she was unhappy because I was gone too much. So I changed my schedule. I took a pay cut to spend more time with her. But she really didn't want that. That's when she left."

"You took a pay cut to be with her? That's really sweet." She grinned in prelude to her next question. "So what do you do when you're not assassinating?"

"Something much less exciting. I sell traffic systems to city and state governments."

"And that's why you're here?"

My answer barely made sense. "Sure."

"How much longer will you be here?"

"Three days."

"Not long," she said. She took a drink, then looked into my eyes. "I'm driving to Salt Lake City tomorrow. Have you ever been there?"

"Just the airport."

"Would you like to come with me?"

The offer surprised me. I wasn't sure how to respond. Aria and I had planned on spending the day together. Lynette must have noticed my hesitation because she quickly said, "I'm sorry, I'm not usually so forward, but Saturday's my only day off and I'm leaving town Sunday evening. I'd like to get to know you better."

I wasn't sure what to do. Finally I said, "I'll make it work. I'd like to get to know you better too."

The rest of the night was pleasant. We talked a lot about Florida, not because I wanted to, but because Lynette did. She had never been to the East Coast. Truthfully, I wanted to tell her about my visits in Midway, but I couldn't figure out any context I could do that in without telling her everything. She was peaceful and I enjoyed every minute being with her. But I still couldn't keep my mind off of Aria.

After dinner I drove Lynette home, then called Aria to change our plans. She didn't answer her phone. Considering her schedule, I'm sure she'd already been asleep for several hours. I didn't want to break our date by voice mail, so I just hung up, planning to call in the morning.

I hoped she'd understand.

Chapter
Thirty

The next morning I woke late because the alarm on my phone didn't go off. I had forgotten to charge it and it had gone dead in the night, which also meant I couldn't call Aria. I plugged it in, then went downstairs to meet Lynette, who had come to join me for breakfast. She was dressed in a form-fitting dark-green sweater with black leggings. She looked beautiful.

As we were eating, Ray walked up to us. "Well, well, now. What a lovely sight." He looked at Lynette. "Hello, my dear."

Lynette stood and the two of them hugged. After she'd sat down, Ray said, "Allow me to vouch for this man. It's been a sheer delight getting to know him."

She smiled at me. "That's good to know."

"Thank you," I said to Ray. "Likewise."

"So what are you kids planning on doing today?"

"We're driving to Salt Lake," Lynette said. "I'm going to show him around."

"That sounds wonderful. Be safe." He winked at me. "Divinity."

The drive to Salt Lake City was pleasant, with natural conversation. Maybe it came from her being a masseuse, or perhaps it was the reason she had become one, but she was easy to talk to. There was no judgment. No hurdles.

When we reached downtown, Lynette directed me to a place called City Creek, an outdoor mall that was festively decorated for the season. Not surprisingly, the mall was crowded.

After wandering around the stores for an hour she said, "Could you excuse me a moment? I need to pick something up."

"Should I go with you?"

"No," she said, smiling. "I'll meet you back here in . . . forty minutes?"

"Sure."

She quickly walked off. I wondered why she didn't want me to go with her. I couldn't imagine she was purchasing something for me.

I found a bench and sat down. I had been people-watching for a few minutes when I spotted a Tiffany jewelry store about fifty yards from me, and I walked to it.

As I wandered around, looking inside their glass showcases, a particular piece caught my eye. It was a quarter-size, white gold pendant in the shape of a star with yellow gems inside.

A saleswoman walked up to me. "May I help you?"

"Could you tell me about that piece? The star one . . ."

"Of course." She reached inside the case and lifted the pendant from its dark blue felt display.

"This piece is called the noble star. The emblem itself is made of white gold. The gems are canary diamond chips."

"Canary diamonds?"

"Yellow diamonds," she said. "They're chips, so they're not faceted."

I looked at the price. It was almost fifteen hundred dollars.

"Would you like to handle it?"

"Yes."

She gingerly handed it to me. "It's really a unique pendant," she said. "I've never seen anything like it."

Neither had I. Chalk it up to my recent insanity, but for some reason I had to buy it. I wasn't even sure who I was buying it for. I assumed it was for LBH. But the truth was, it was Aria who kept coming to mind.

Lynette was waiting for me as I walked back. She was now carrying several large shopping bags. I should have known that the robin's-egg-blue Tiffany sack would catch her attention.

"You bought something at Tiffany?"

I glanced down at the small sack. "Yes. For a friend."

She didn't say anything.

Afterward we drove to the Grand America Hotel. We had lunch at the elegant Garden Café, then followed their holiday "window stroll," a tour of the hotel's Christmas-themed windows, culminating in a life-size gingerbread house that allegedly had taken thirteen hundred pounds of flour, three hundred pounds of sugar, and fifteen hundred eggs to make.

All day long I waited for the right time to tell Lynette that I'd been reading her blog and why I had really come to Utah, but the right time never came. We concluded our day with dinner at a restaurant that overlooked the impressively illuminated Temple Square. Afterward we went to see the grounds.

The air was cold but not as brisk as in Midway. As we walked, Lynette moved close to me, and I could tell that she wanted to hold hands. I took her hand, though, for some reason, it felt a little unnatural.

She was quiet. We both were. It had been a nice day. A pleasant day. But something felt wrong. Maybe that it was nice and pleasant and nothing but that was exactly what was wrong. I had expected something more from meeting LBH—something magical and passionate. Instead the day felt like a pleasant outing with a good friend. Or a sister.

Lynette didn't say much until we were nearly to the mouth of the canyon.

"Thank you for today. It was really nice."

"It was my pleasure. Thank you for the invitation."

She looked over at me. "I wish you weren't leaving town so soon."

"Me too," I said.

The silence boomed. I wasn't sure what to say. Then she said, "Would you like to come over for lunch tomorrow?"

"I thought you were leaving town."

"Tomorrow night. But if you already have other plans . . ."

I didn't have plans. At least not yet. "No, that sounds nice. What time should I come?"

"Two?"

"Two it is."

Even though I was missing Aria, I had to go. It was my last chance to tell her why I was really there. It was my last chance to confront LBH.

When I got back to my room I picked up my phone, afraid of what I'd find. There were six voice-mail messages—one from Nate, one from Dale, the other four from Aria. I felt a sharp stab of guilt.

I listened to Nate's and Dale's messages first just to get them out of the way. Nate was characteristically succinct.

It's Nate, call me back.

Dale wasn't so succinct.

Hey, dude, it's Dale, returning your call. Don't know what you need. Maybe you got married. If it was just a butt call, this never happened. Call me anyway.

I selected the first of Aria's messages. Her voice started out bright and happy and fell with each succeeding call.

9:17 - Hi, Alex. It's Aria. I saw that you called last night, sorry I went to bed the second I got home. I was so tired. So, I was just checking to see if we're still on for today. I missed seeing you yesterday. . . . Looking forward to seeing you.

9:56 - Hi, it's me again. Aria. I don't know if you got my last message. Please call when you get a chance. Let me know what's going on.

12:16 - Hi, it's Aria. I don't know what's going on. If I did something to offend you, I'm sorry. Please call me.

On her last message her voice was soft and painful. Vulnerable.

4:36 - Hi. I don't know if you're trying to say good-bye without talking to me. I guess you are, right? My heart hurts. I really liked being with you. I don't know what I did, or if you just realized that you didn't want to be with me. . . . Anyway, I know you'll be leaving soon and I just wanted to tell you that it was nice getting to know you. I wish you well.

Her voice rang off with sadness. My heart ached. I immediately called her back but she didn't answer. Her phone must have been turned off or maybe I was blocked, because it wouldn't even allow me to leave a message. How stupid could I be?

Chapter
Thirty-one

I didn't sleep well. I had dreams about Aria. I felt like I had dozens of them, but I only remembered one. It was disturbing. Lynette was putting a black bag over Aria's head. Before she did, Aria looked up at me. Her eyes turned to stone.

I didn't know if Aria was working or not, and I didn't want to wake her if she wasn't, so I waited until nine to call her. She didn't answer. I called again. And again.

Then Lynette texted me to ask me how I liked my steak.

I texted back.

Medium well. I'll see you soon.

Finally I called Nate. He didn't answer, and I figured he was probably at church, so I called Dale. He answered on the second ring.

"Hey, man. When did you get back?"

"I'm not. I'm still in Utah."

"Still in Utah? Can't find her?"

"No, I found her. But I've got a problem."

"She's *married*. She's a *he*. She's *ugleeeee* . . ."

"Stop," I said. "No, it's . . . I came out here for one woman and I found two."

Dale was quiet for just a moment, then burst out laughing.

"Stop laughing," I said. "Not everything's a joke."

"I'm sorry, man. I'm not laughing at you, I'm laughing with the universe. I think it's great."

"It's not *great*. It's a problem."

"You fell in love with two women in, like, a week?"

"No. I fell in love with Lynette months ago. But there's another woman . . . It's like . . ." I didn't know how to describe Aria.

"Speechless. I love it. Wait, I've got the answer. You're in Utah; they do that *Big Love* thing out there. Bring them both back."

"Stop it," I said.

"Look, lighten up, man. You sound like you have an actual problem, like third-world debt or world hunger. Your problem is a good problem. What's better than having two potential clients competing for your sale? You just take the highest bidder. And in this case, by *highest bidder* I mean the largest bra size."

"I'm hanging up."

"I can't wait to meet her."

I hung up. I sat there for a minute, then went to the counter and retrieved the dried edelweiss that Ray had given me. I looked around for something to put it in. The only thing I could find, besides the room's laundry bag, was the Tiffany bag. I took the pendant out and hid it inside my suitcase, then put the edelweiss in the bag.

I know, in hindsight, I should have known better. It was a man-dumb thing.

On the drive over to Lynette's my mind was going faster than the car, which wasn't surprising, since the roads were like tundra and I had to drive as slow as a Miami retiree to keep from going into a ditch.

The same worry played over and over in my mind. *How will she respond once she knows the truth about why I'm here?*

When I got to the house I rang the doorbell. Lynette greeted me with a hug. "I'm so glad to see you again."

"Me too."

She looked down at the Tiffany bag but said nothing about it. "Come in; everything's ready."

I followed her into the dining room. The food was already on the table. "Let's eat," she said.

Everything was delicious, and we didn't talk much. After a few minutes, she said, "You're quiet today."

I looked up and smiled. "It's a good sign. I'm always quiet when there's good food."

"Thank you."

The truth was, my mind was still shuffling through the deck of possible outcomes I was about to face. How would she respond to my stalking her? How would she respond to the edelweiss? Was it as big a deal as she'd said in her blog? What if it was too big a deal? What if she took it as a proposal? Was it one? I began to question the wisdom of giving her the flower. Still, she'd already seen the bag. I was committed.

"So, where are you off to tonight?" I asked, trying to fill the silence.

"I'm going to a soul restoration camp in Star, Idaho," she said.

"Soul restoration?"

She nodded. "It's part of a community of women I belong to called Brave Girls Club."

"Are you brave?" I asked.

"I try to be."

When we'd finished our meal she brought over a chocolate Bundt cake and started cutting it. "You're going to have to take the rest back to the inn with you. It won't be good when I get back."

"I'll share it with Ray," I said.

"He'll be happy." She handed me a plate, then looked at me with a serene smile. It was time.

"I have something for you," I said. I lifted the Tiffany bag. Her face lit with excitement. Then I took out the edelweiss and handed it to her. She looked down at my gift, then back at me. Her expression had changed from happiness to confusion. Or maybe disappointment.

"Thank you," she finally said.

Her response wasn't what I expected. "It's edelweiss."

She hesitated a moment and then said, "It's pretty."

"It's pretty?"

She laughed. "Yes, it's pretty." A moment later she added, "Is something wrong with that?"

"No. I just expected . . . more." (Looking back, I'm sure she was thinking the same.)

"I'm sorry. I like it. I especially like that you brought me a flower."

I looked at her quizzically. "Didn't your father once tell you something special about edelweiss?"

"My father? No. How do you know my father?"

"Is your father German?"

"My father's French. Bucher is a French surname."

I just gazed at her for a moment, then said, "Did you know that being lonely actually drops your body temperature?"

Now she looked at me as if I'd just lost my mind. Maybe I had. "Why did you just ask me that?"

"You're not her," I said.

"I'm not who?"

"You're not the one I came here for."

She looked upset. "I don't understand. You came here looking for someone?"

I stood. "I'm so sorry. I've made a very big mistake."

Chapter
Thirty-two

On the way from Lynette's house I called Aria again, but there was still no answer. I drove across town to the diner and hurried inside. The restaurant wasn't crowded, just four tables of customers, but I couldn't see Aria anywhere.

The older waitress, Valerie, had glanced over at me as I walked in, but she didn't seem to be in much of a hurry to help me. She finished talking to some diners, then casually walked over to me. "What can I do for you?" Her voice was hard.

"Is Aria here?"

"No, she's not."

"Did she work today?"

"No, she didn't."

"Do you know where she is?"

"Why would I know that?"

Talking to her was like pulling thistles with bare hands. Finally I said, "All right. When you see her, please tell her I came by."

She didn't speak for a moment, and then she said, "I don't think I will."

"Excuse me?"

"I don't think I will. Let me tell you something about Aria. She's one of the sweetest people I've ever known. She's like a delicate piece of porcelain, precious but fragile. But a big-city man like you doesn't care about things like that. She was supposed to be working today, but she called in sick last night. I don't remember the last time she called in sick. It's been years. I could tell she'd been crying. I pressed her, and she told me that you had stood her up.

"Maybe it's okay to treat women like that where you come from, but here it's not." Her eyes squinted until they were almost closed, and she jabbed at me with her finger. "So you listen well, big city. If you're going to contact her again, and I hope you don't, but if you do, you better be good to her. Aria's got a lot of big men with little brains who would like nothing more than to earn a few brownie points by defending her honor—if you catch my drift."

"I catch your drift," I said. "And no, I don't believe in treating women that way. Things happened that were out of my control. I'm trying to find her to apologize."

"Yeah, well, you do that. And you watch your back. We small towns have our ways."

In one sentence she had gone from *Steel Magnolias* to *Deliverance*.

I drove directly to Aria's house. Her Jeep was parked in front, but the house lights were out. I walked up and pounded on the door. "Aria."

She didn't answer. I tried calling her on the

phone again, but my call still didn't go through. I pounded again. "Aria!"

After several minutes of pounding I heard footsteps inside. The door opened slowly, slightly, the security chain still attached. Aria looked at me through the crack. "What do you want?"

"I am so sorry. I tried to call you. I called you Friday night. I tried to call you as soon as I got your messages."

She didn't say anything.

"Can we talk?"

"No."

"May I explain?"

She looked at me for a moment, then said, "You have one minute."

"Out here?"

"Where were you Saturday?"

"I'm so sorry. I had to finish the search. That's why I came here. I thought I found her."

"And did you?"

"I thought I did. But it wasn't her. I made a mistake."

"And if she had been LBH, you never would have come back?"

"I would have come back. I couldn't stop thinking of you. I promise. Please give me another chance. I want to be with you. I still want to get that Christmas tree with you."

"Saturday was my only day off."

"Then we'll go after your shift."

"You leave tomorrow."

"I'll extend my stay."

She just looked at me angrily. Then she said, "Why would you do that?"

Her words stung. For a moment I was speechless. I couldn't believe how quickly I had messed up something so beautiful. Finally I said, "I'm sorry. I thought you might want me to." I took a deep breath. "I'm really sorry. More than you'll ever know. I think you're really wonderful and brave. I loved getting to know you. I was hoping to get to know you even better." I took another deep breath. "I'll leave you alone." I turned and began to walk away.

As I stepped off the porch, Aria shouted, "Did you get a permit?"

I turned back. "What?"

"You need a permit to cut down a tree."

"No."

"Get one. Tomorrow." She shut the door.

"Okay," I said to the closed door. "I'll get a permit."

Chapter
Thirty-three

As soon as I got back to the inn, I stopped at the front desk to extend my stay. The Shakespeare Room wasn't available on the twenty-sixth, so they moved me to the Jane Austen Room. I didn't care.

I walked up the stairs to my room and went right to bed. Frankly, I felt like I'd messed up more lives in this little town in the last week than I had in the last decade in Daytona Beach. I felt awful about leaving Lynette like that. She deserved better. Maybe someday I'd explain it to her, though I doubted she'd ever speak to me again. At least she was on her way to a Brave Girls soul retreat or whatever it was called. I'm sure those women would have a lot to say about me and my Tiffany bag of dried edelweiss.

Still, she had played an important role in my journey. I realized that I no longer cared about finding LBH. I was just grateful that Aria had given me a second chance.

The next morning I spent nearly forty minutes changing my flights home. Then I dressed and went downstairs to eat a light breakfast of oatmeal with milk, brown sugar, and walnuts, then headed off to get my tree-cutting permit.

To my dismay, Ray had told me that I'd have to go back to the mayor's office.

I considered myself fortunate that he didn't ask me about Lynette. I wouldn't have even known where to start. I felt bad that he had personally vouched for me. I hoped I hadn't jeopardized their relationship. Or at least his monthly massages.

As I walked into the city office, the mayor remembered me.

"You're back."

"I'd like a permit to cut a Christmas tree. Am I at the right place?"

"You would like permission to kill one of our trees."

"Yes, ma'am. Mayor."

"And you still haven't killed any of my constituency?"

"Not that I'm aware of."

She eyed me for a moment more, then said, "I will grant you a permit." She bent over and scribbled on a form. Then she looked up and said, "That will be ten dollars."

I gave her cash and she handed me the permit, a receipt, and a paper with the rules of tree cutting.

"Have a nice day," I said.

"You too, Mr. Pear."

I didn't know if she was mocking me or if she had just confused me with one of the murder suspects in the board game Clue.

With my permit in hand, I drove into Heber for

Christmas tree decorations. The only place I could find Christmas paraphernalia was a grocery store called, appropriately, The Store, and an Ace Hardware.

At The Store, I bought several boxes of colored lights, baubles, and tinsel. I also bought a package of mistletoe, hoping it might come in handy as a tension breaker. Or, worst case, to replace the prehistoric sprig of mistletoe hanging in the front of the diner.

Drew, the guy at the hardware store, took a proactive role in helping me prepare for my tree-cutting outing. He either sensed that I needed help or, more likely, since I was the only one in the store, he needed the sales. He never left my side.

Drew sold me a festive red-and-green metal tree stand, fifty feet of nylon rope to tie the tree to my car with, and a very expensive handsaw to cut the tree, as well as work gloves to handle the very expensive handsaw. He also tried to sell me a tarp to protect my car from the tree, but that's where I drew the line.

Sometimes it takes a salesman to appreciate a good salesman. Drew was a good salesman. Our *free* tree was getting expensive.

By the time I finished my purchases, it was a little past noon. As I drove over to the diner to see Aria, I was pretty anxious. I had no idea how she was going to respond. It wasn't like we had had much of a talk through the crack in the door. I never even really saw all of her face— at least not all of it at the same time. Yes, I had apologized, but I didn't know to what extent she had accepted it. I hoped that she hadn't changed her mind. I wouldn't blame her if she had, but I hoped.

I walked into the diner to the Carpenters' "I'll Be Home for Christmas" playing on the jukebox. To my dismay, Valerie was standing at the front counter. When she saw me, her expression abruptly changed from a smile to a scowl.

"Hi, Valerie."

She glared at me, then said in a low grumble, "I'll tell her you're here."

She walked around to the kitchen, and a moment later Aria walked out. She looked at me with an expression that was difficult to read. Noticeably, she didn't hug me. But, in fairness, she didn't slap me either.

"Hi," I said.

"Hi," she echoed.

I swayed nervously on the balls of my feet. "I got our permit. And decorations. And baubles and lights and tinsel. And a saw. And gloves. And a rope . . ."

To my relief she smiled. "I have a saw."

"I can take mine back," I said. "It was expensive."

"Thank you. Would you like some lunch?"

"I . . ."

"Say yes."

"Yes. I'd love some lunch."

"Your booth's open. Seat yourself; I'll be right over."

I grabbed a menu, walked over to the booth, and sat down. Aria came over a few minutes later.

"How's your day?" I asked.

"Better than yesterday. Thank you for coming over last night. I was really hurt."

"I'm so very, very sorry."

"I know. You were sweet last night. And cute."

"As long as you know I was sorry."

"I do. And I understand. Now, what can I get you to eat?"

I ordered a Reuben sandwich and a bowl of vegetable beef soup. At the risk of offending Thelma, I passed on peach pie. Before leaving, I asked Aria what time she was off.

"I was supposed to work until nine, but Valerie said she'd work late for me. So I'm off at three."

I was surprised to hear this; maybe even a little suspicious. "Valerie offered to work for you so you could go out with me?"

"Yes. You should thank her."

"I'll pass on that," I said. "Valerie's not really a fan."

"Of course she is. She's just teasing you."

"No. She's not. She scares me a little."

Aria smiled. "Valerie scares you?"

"A little."

"Well, she bought your lunch for you."

I looked at my food, then back at her. "Are you sure she didn't poison it?"

"She never touched it."

"She's a very complex woman," I said. "I'll be back at three." I got up to leave, then said, "Aria, do something for me."

"What's that?"

"Wait for me *inside* the diner."

She smiled, kissed me on the cheek, and then walked away. I looked over, and Valerie again glared at me. Then she pointed. She was very complex.

I returned to the diner a little before three. Aria was standing outside, but only because she saw me pull into the parking lot. She had changed from her waitress outfit and was wearing a parka, high boots, and a red Santa Claus cap.

"Ready for this?" she asked as she climbed into my car.

"You know," I said, "this is a bucket-list moment for me. I've wanted to cut down my own Christmas tree since I was a kid. It just always looked like so much fun on those coffee commercials."

She smiled. "I'm glad."

"Where do we go?"

"We're headed back over by the hot pot. Do you remember how to get there?"

"I might need some help."

I drove the route we had followed before, though she had to show me where the turnoff was. We continued about a half mile past the hot pot, which was easy to see with the steam rising off it. I kind of expected to see Cal watching us with binoculars. Or his shotgun.

"Is this all your rancher's property?" I asked.

"This part is, but where we're going isn't. Otherwise we wouldn't have needed a permit."

"Why don't we just take one of his trees?"

"He never offered."

We drove on, snaking our way back and forth to the top of the mountain, which, incidentally, Aria referred to as a *hill,* not a mountain. The depth of the snow around us increased as we climbed in altitude, but the road was clear. Finally she said, "This is the place."

I parked on the side of the snowbanked road and we got out. We had forgotten to go back to Aria's to get her saw, so I had to unwrap my new one, rendering it unreturnable. At least I had a souvenir to commemorate the day.

The top of the mountain—actually, the whole mountain—was covered with trees, though most of them were much larger than we could use. It took us almost a half hour wading through knee-high snow to find the right one.

There were rules to this tree-cutting business. We could only take subalpine fir trees—*Abies lasiocarpa*—that were twenty feet high or shorter. I had no idea what a subalpine fir was—actually, I didn't know the difference between a fir and a spruce—but the paper said that we could recognize the tree by its needles, which were blunt and tended to turn upward. Fortunately, Aria didn't need the paper to find the right kind of tree; she knew exactly what we were looking for.

We picked out a tree about seven feet high, well shaped, with only one bare spot, which Aria said she would turn toward the wall.

I kicked the snow from the base of the tree, then took my saw to its trunk. I tried to make sawing through it look easy. *It wasn't easy.* Aria patiently watched as I sawed and sawed and sawed my way through the base. She clapped when the tree finally fell. I dragged our subalpine fir back to the car, leaving a hundred-yard-long furrow in the virgin snow.

We tied the tree to the roof of my Ford with my fifty feet of nylon rope and drove back to Aria's, where we untied it and carried it to her front porch. I didn't need to brush any snow off the tree, as the drive back had done that for us.

While I carried the tree in, Aria set up the stand in the corner of her front room. It took several tries to get the tree into the stand, but I eventually did, with the bare spot facing the wall, and we clamped it in place. The tree fit nicely in the corner, and we sat on the floor to admire it. Then I got the decorations from my car and we strung the lighting first, and then, one by one, the baubles.

As Aria went through the sack of decorations, she lifted out the package of mistletoe. "What's this for?"

I looked at her innocently, then shrugged. "It's a secret."

"A mistletoe secret." She opened the package and put the sprig in her hair. Then she took my hand and pulled me over to the couch. We didn't finish the tree for several hours after that.

Chapter
Thirty-four

"I know what we should do tomorrow," Aria said, rolling off me. The room was dark, lit only by the colorful flashing lights of the Christmas tree.

"More of this," I said.

"No. I mean, yes, of course, but we can't do this *all* day."

"You have all day?"

"I got tomorrow off."

"You said you had to work."

"I can work any day. But how often do I get you?"

I went to kiss her again, but, still smiling, she pushed me away. "Hold on. So, about tomorrow. As long as you're in Utah, I think we should go skiing."

"Snow skiing?"

She rolled her eyes. "No, waterskiing."

"I've never skied before. Not a lot of opportunity in central Florida."

"So?"

"You'll teach me?"

"No. But I'll enroll you in a class and come with you to laugh."

"I can't wait."

"It's a date," she said.

• • •

The next morning I picked Aria up at eight o'clock. We stopped by the diner for coffee, biscuits, and eggs, then headed off to Deer Valley Resort, which was a bit more expensive than Park City but less crowded.

I took a two-hour lesson with a bunch of kids (except for a teenager from Jamaica, I was the only one older than seven), then we went up on the slopes. I didn't look cool, but I only fell twice on the beginner hills and, at the end of the day, went down an intermediate hill with Aria without killing myself. She made it look pretty easy, and I assumed that she was an expert.

By four o'clock we were exhausted—at least I was—and we returned my skis, then I treated her to dinner at the lodge.

After we had ordered I asked, "Have you ever skied the black diamond?"

She nodded. "Yes, but I don't like working that hard."

"So you do this a lot?"

"Rarely."

"Why's that?"

She looked at me as if she was surprised I didn't know. "I'm a girl of limited means."

At that moment I remembered the Tiffany pendant I'd bought in Salt Lake City. "May I give you something for Christmas?" I asked.

She smiled. "Yes. If I can give you something."

"Fair enough."

"I know what I want," she said. "If you can afford it."

"Try me."

"I want to spend Christmas with you."

After dinner we drove back to Midway. We went back to her house for coffee and ended up on the couch in front of the tree. Aria was quiet for a little while, then set down her coffee. "May I ask you something?"

"Of course."

"You said you're done looking for LBH. And you had made a mistake."

"Yes."

"What happened?"

"Do you really want to know?"

She nodded.

"Okay," I said. "Do you know someone named Lynette Hurt?"

"Yes, she's a massage therapist over by the community center. I went to her a while back when I hurt my shoulder." She thought a moment, then said, "Lynette Hurt. Lynette *Bucher* Hurt. LBH. You thought it was her."

"Yes. And Ray thought it was her. He was the one who told me about her. When I went to see her I found out that she was leaving town, so it was my only chance to really check her out."

Aria cocked her head. "Check her out?"

"In a manner of speaking," I said.

"She *is* pretty," Aria said.

"I didn't notice."

"Yeah, right." Aria took another sip of coffee and then said, "So how did you know it wasn't her?"

"I gave her edelweiss."

To my surprise, Aria's expression abruptly changed. She was quiet for a moment, then she said, "You gave her edelweiss?"

"Yeah. But it meant nothing to her. Edelweiss was an important thing to the real LBH."

Suddenly Aria's eyes welled up with tears.

"Why are you crying?" I asked softly. When she didn't answer, I said, "I'm sorry, it didn't mean anything to me. I just had to know if it was her . . ."

Tears began to fall down Aria's cheeks. Suddenly it was as if a curtain had been pulled back from my mind. I understood. "You're LBH."

Aria just looked at me. She looked afraid.

"Aria."

Nothing.

"Aria, who is LBH?"

"I don't know."

"Aria, tell me."

"I don't know!" she shouted.

I could feel my face turning red. "What are you hiding from me? Who is LBH?"

"She's someone you said you cared about."

"Aria!"

She looked at me, then shouted, "Lonely Broken Heart, okay? Are you happy?"

I stood. Something she said had flipped some subconscious trigger. I felt my skin turn hot. I felt something crashing inside me, like the moment I found the note from Clark in Jill's pants.

"You've been lying to me. You knew I was looking for you. You knew this whole time."

"I didn't know this whole time. I didn't know until you told me you were looking for LBH. I was already in love with you."

"You said you didn't know who she was."

"You asked me if I knew anyone with those initials. I didn't. I told you the truth."

"That's not the truth. You knew what I was really asking. You knew, and you deceived me. Just like Jill. You're no different than Jill." I put my hand on my forehead and walked to the side of the room. I felt like a madman. I *was* a madman. It was as if my brain had been hijacked by my deepest fears.

"I've spent the last five years listening to lies and secrets. All I wanted from you was honesty. I fell in love with LBH because she was honest. And you gave me more lies."

"Please don't make me pay for what your wife did. What was I supposed to do?"

I spun around. "You were supposed to tell me the truth! Was that asking too much?"

Aria began sobbing. "I wanted to. But I was afraid. I was afraid I might lose you."

"For telling the truth? It's not the truth—it's the lies that get you into trouble. Just like when you lied to the police about your father!"

I regretted the words even before they came out of my mouth. Aria froze. It was as if I'd slugged her. I suppose I had done worse than that. For a moment she couldn't talk. She couldn't even breathe. Then she fell forward to her knees, holding her sides and shaking. Without looking at me, she said, "Please leave. Please leave me. Please don't ever come back."

I felt sick. I wished I could take the words back, but it was too late. I had said too much. Strikes two and three, and I was out. I looked at her for a moment, then turned and walked out the door. *What had I done?*

Chapter

Thirty-five

It was the twenty-third of December, the busiest travel day of the season and second-busiest travel day of the year. Trying to get back home was a nightmare. I first tried to book a flight to Daytona Beach, but came up with nothing. Then Florida. Then I looked for *anything* out of Utah. Every seat out of Salt Lake International was full with confirmed oversales. I should have known better. I couldn't have picked a worse time for my world to collapse.

Fate may have kept me in Utah, but I didn't have to stay in Midway. I couldn't stay in Midway. It was as if the air in the city had dissipated. The proximity to Aria was killing me. Early the next morning I found a hotel vacancy near the airport and booked a room. By nine I carried my bag downstairs to check out. Ray was in the dining room, visiting with some guests, when he noticed me standing at the front desk with my suitcase. He immediately jumped up and rushed to me, his face bent with distress.

"Alex, are you leaving us?"

"Yes, sir."

"I thought you were staying until after

Christmas. I hoped to share some more time with you."

"I had planned on it. But . . . something came up."

He carefully studied my countenance, his face mirroring the pain and sadness in mine. "I'm sorry you didn't find what you were looking for."

"No," I said. "The problem is, I did."

He put his hand on my shoulder. "No, my friend. You most certainly did not find what you were looking for."

I looked back into his eyes for a moment, then said, "Thanks for everything. It was a pleasure getting to know you."

"I've grown rather fond of you, young man. I hope to see you again."

Then he turned and walked back to the dining room.

I went back to the front counter. Lita smiled at me sadly. "We're sorry to see you go, Mr. Bartlett. I hope you've had a memorable visit."

"Most definitely memorable," I said. I handed her my key. "Thanks for everything."

"Merry Christmas. It's been a pleasure having you with us."

"Thank you, Lita. The same to you."

I couldn't leave the small town fast enough. When I reached Salt Lake I checked in at the hotel, then drove to the airport to return my rental car. I was glad I was dropping off, not picking up. The lines at the rental car service were obscene. Actually, the lines everywhere were obscene, the mobs uniting for the holiday. Once again, I was going against the traffic.

Chapter
Thirty-six

I ended up taking a taxi back to my hotel even though it was only a mile from the airport. It wasn't the distance, it was the traffic. Airport grounds aren't really designed for pedestrians. My cabdriver was already in a sour mood, made more so by my minimal fare. I left him a twenty-dollar tip to stop his grumbling.

In the ninety minutes I'd been gone, the hotel's population had grown considerably, and the lobby was crowded. Ironically, it was there, in the crush of the crowd, that my mistress Loneliness finally caught up with me again. Maybe she had always been with me and I'd just been too distracted by my quest to notice her soft footsteps or to hear her familiar whisperings, but I heard them now. *"Don't worry that you have no one, Alex; I'm here for you. You'll always have me. I'll never leave you . . ."*

Where do all these tribes come from? I thought. Then I realized that I had regurgitated a line from LBH. Funny thing; in my mind I continued to keep separate the two beings—Aria and LBH—as if my heart still hadn't reconciled that they were one. I suppose it was emotionally safer that way.

I retrieved my bag from the bell stand and went up to my room. I checked on flights again. There was no direct flight to Daytona Beach, but there was a flight the next morning at 8:17 to Atlanta and, after a four-hour layover, another flight to Jacksonville—an hour and a half from Daytona. I didn't care what the cab ride cost. I just wanted to be home.

When I was in second grade, a girl brought a robin's egg she'd found in her yard for show and tell. Our teacher had put a sign next to it saying DO NOT TOUCH. I was just seven years old, so, of course, I had to touch it. To my horror, it broke. I looked around to see if anyone had seen what I'd done, and then I quickly crept back to my desk where no one could connect me with the broken egg. Right now was no different. I just wanted to be far away from the mess I'd made in Utah.

Chapter
Thirty-seven

I woke the next morning at six. I suppose it was telling that I had set two wake-up calls, my phone's alarm clock and the alarm clock in the room. I wasn't taking any chances on missing my flight. Nothing short of a terrorist attack was going to keep me in Utah.

After I'd boarded the plane I checked my phone. To be honest, there was a small part of me that hoped Aria had called. It was good she hadn't. I wasn't ready for it. Even after we screw up, it's amazing the lengths our psyches will go to protect our egos. *She lied,* it screamed at me. *You did the right thing. When you pick up one end of the stick, you pick up the other. In the end, it would finish with a lie, just like it did before. Just like it did when you tried to pretend lies don't matter. Just like it did with Jill.*

As I looked at my phone I noticed that someone had left a message. It had a Daytona Beach area code, but I didn't recognize the number. I pushed Play.

Alex, it's Jill. I'm probably the last person you expected to hear from, but I just wanted to wish you a Merry Christmas. I came by a little earlier, but it didn't look like you were home. Or maybe you were home and were hiding from me. I wouldn't blame you. But it is the season, right? If you'll let me know when you'll be there, I'll come by again. I have something for you. A little Christmas gift. [Pause] Okay, well, take care. 'Bye.

What did she want? I turned off my phone. I didn't want to talk to anyone. With my Diamond Medallion status I was almost always upgraded to first class or, at the least, coach comfort, but not this time. For the four hours of the flight to Atlanta, I didn't even have a decent coach seat. I sat in the middle seat between two overfed men and directly behind a crying baby. I was certain it was just the universe's way of punishing me for what I'd done.

When we finally reached Atlanta I camped out in the Crown Room. Still, the wait seemed interminable. I never turned on my phone. I still didn't want to talk to anyone. I didn't want anyone to know that I was back.

I was upgraded to first class on my flight to Jacksonville, which was no big deal, since the flight was less than an hour, and then I waited forty minutes for my bag and another thirty minutes for a cab.

The driver played Christmas music in the car for the entire ninety-minute ride. It already seemed strange to look out the window and not see snow.

With the two-hour time change, I arrived home past midnight. I paid the driver, then started into my apartment when he yelled, "Hey!"

I turned back.

"Merry Christmas."

"Yeah," I said. *Freaking Merry Christmas.*

I now understood why suicides go up during the holidays.

Chapter
Thirty-eight

I woke the next day about noon. Christmas Day. I lay in bed with the blinds down for more than an hour. The world outside my bed offered me nothing. It was weird being back—surreal, like I'd just woken from a dream. Actually, a nightmare.

I didn't care that it was Christmas. The more tragic commemoration was that it was almost the anniversary of my divorce. It had gone through on the twenty-seventh of December. I wondered if that had something to do with why Jill had called.

I felt like my chest had been run over by a semi. Not just my chest—my whole body. My back and neck ached. Even my feet ached. How can depression make your feet ache?

I was in so much pain that I went for a bottle of Jack Daniel's, but I put it back, not out of wisdom or temperance but out of self-hate. *How dare I run from what I brought on myself? I deserve to hurt.* Though outwardly I still blamed her, my inner self knew the truth. Ray had told me she was a flickering flame about to go out. What had Valerie called her? *A precious, fragile thing.* I had blown out a candle. I had broken a precious, fragile thing. I deserved to pay for what I had done. I didn't know how I could.

● ● ●

I stayed in bed for the next two days. I kept my phone off, as if it would release me from liability that way. I didn't shower. My beard began to grow. I was a mess.

It was late Sunday night, two days after Christmas, when Nate knocked on my door. I didn't know it was Nate; I just knew someone was pounding on my door with the force of a battering ram. Actually, he was hitting my door with the business end of his cane. Then I heard him shout, "Open up, man. I know you're home."

I wondered how he knew that, as there was no outward sign of life. When I wasn't sleeping I had been watching all five seasons of *Breaking Bad*. I was ready to run off to New Mexico and open a meth lab. I opened the door.

"So you are alive," he said. He looked me over. "I think."

"I'm not in a mood to talk," I said.

"I can see that. That's why we're going to." He walked into my house and into my TV room, where he sat down on my couch. I followed him and settled into a recliner across from him.

"When did you get back?"

I sighed heavily. "Christmas Eve."

He looked at me incredulously. "And you didn't call? What's going on? Dale told me that you found her."

"I thought I had."

"So you didn't find her."

"No, I did."

"You're talking in circles, man."

"While I was looking, I fell in love with a woman. Aria . . ."

"That's her name? Aria?"

"Yeah."

"Pretty name," he said.

I didn't want to hear that. "It turned out that Aria was really LBH."

"You accidentally ran into the woman you were looking for?"

"Yes."

"That's incredible."

"It's not incredible. She knew I was looking for her and she played me."

Nate looked at me unsympathetically. "Played you? What does that mean?"

"She *lied* to me. She pretended to be someone she wasn't."

"Who did she pretend to be?"

"Not LBH."

"And, so, now you're upset with her?"

"Of course I am."

He thought for a moment, then said, "And you told her up front exactly what you were up to?"

"No. It would have freaked her out."

He looked at me as if I were dumb. "Have

you considered that maybe that's how *she* felt?"

I didn't answer. He leaned forward. "Look, man. This was your crazy idea, not hers. You got to read her blog posts and get to know her intimately before you even met. Didn't she have the right to get to know you, in a safe place too?"

Again I didn't answer him.

"Honestly, man. What was she supposed to do?"

I blew up. "She was supposed to be honest."

Nate didn't even flinch. I suppose, compared to mortar fire and IEDs, my tirade wasn't much. "Under normal circumstances, you'd be right," he said calmly. "But these weren't normal circumstances, were they? You flew to Utah to track down someone you didn't know without telling them what you were doing. You said it yourself—that's crazy stuff. And crazy people do crazy stuff. She would have been a fool to tell you who she was." He leaned forward. "Be honest, here. Are you fighting her or are you fighting Jill? Because she's not Jill, and she deserves a fresh slate, just like you do. The past is a lesson, not a sentence. Let it go."

"I don't get why you're taking her side. You don't even know her."

He looked at me with an amused grin. "You think I'm taking her side?" When I didn't answer he said, "You're right, I don't know her. I couldn't pick her out of a police lineup. I'm not doing this for someone I don't know, I'm doing this for you."

"Why do you think you know what's right for me?"

"Because I remember what you said before you left. You told me that you knew deep in your heart you had to find her. You knew."

I looked down for a moment, then said, "I was wrong. The inspiration was wrong. It was just hopeful thinking. I wanted to believe something good was out there."

Nate just looked at me quietly, and then said, "Did I ever tell you about how I got so broken up?"

"You ran over an IED."

"Yeah," he said. "I did. Twice. You think that's unlucky?"

"I'd say so."

"You're wrong. I'm the luckiest man alive. The second time I hit the mine was my fifty-ninth mission. I had just landed up in Sulaymaniyah, near the Kurdish region.

"When we hit dirt I was ordered to report immediately to the CO for action. The CO there had a reputation for being a belligerent SOB. He always made it a point to rip some unlucky guy a new one before each mission, just to keep everyone else on their toes.

"As I ran to the CO's tent I had this overwhelming urge to stop in the worship tent. Every camp has a worship tent. It has icons and religious stuff. The thing is, I had never even been in a worship tent. I wasn't religious. I thought religion was nothing more than a crutch, and Marines don't need crutches. We put people in them. Or graves.

"Trust me, I had no delusion that there was some good-time afterlife party waiting for me. My sergeant in basic drilled it into us. He said, 'You're all going to hell. Get used to it. The only comfort is, you've already been there, so it's no big deal.' After some of the things I'd done, I was pretty damn certain I wasn't on God's friends and family plan.

"But here I am walking to the worship tent. I thought, *This is insane,* but the feeling was unlike anything I'd felt before.

"I went inside and I didn't even know what to do, so I did what I thought I should do. I knelt down and started to pray. I didn't know how to, so I just started talking.

"Next thing I know, I check my watch. I'd been there for almost thirty minutes. *Thirty minutes.* The CO was going to rip off my head and shove it down my throat.

"I jumped up to go, but as I went to leave I saw this little metal cross lying on a table—it was a Celtic cross. I didn't know what it was called at the time, I just knew it was a cross with a circle in the middle. The same voice that sent me to the tent said to me, 'Take it.'

"I thought, *I can't take it. It belongs to the tent.* The voice said again, 'Take it.'

"I resisted. *This is crazy,* I told myself. *I'm talking to myself.* I went to leave the tent when that voice inside said, 'Don't leave without it.' You could say it was my subconscious, but I swear that whatever I was hearing had an authority my own thoughts never had. It felt like an order. So I grabbed the cross, shoved it into my pocket, and walked out.

"Just as I feared, when I hit the CO's tent he was waiting for me. He ripped me up one side and down the other in front of the whole squad. He said I'd held up the war for forty minutes and he was going to take it out of my flesh when I got back. Then he sent us off.

"Two hours later, we're coming to this little village when we hit an IED. Our Humvee was blown to pieces. When I came to, I was lying on my back bleeding from a hundred places. My back was broken. My hip was torn wide open. My buddies were also blown up. One of them was next to me, shaking.

"The enemy was firing missiles and machine guns at us from a nearby building. I couldn't move. I knew it was over. As I lay there waiting to die, I suddenly felt the cross burning in my pocket. I reached down for it. It was covered with blood. I held it to my chest, waiting to be overrun by our enemy.

"Then out of the corner of my eye I saw a cloud of dust coming toward us. I wasn't sure what it was I saw, but I knew it couldn't be good. Suddenly it started firing. But not at us. It was an M1 Abrams, a US tank. It parked itself between us and harm's way, then proceeded to take out the whole of the enemy.

"I just lay there listening to the battle, tears rolling down my cheeks, not because I was in pain but because I knew this was impossible. We had no backup. There was no cavalry in the area. That tank came out of nowhere to save our lives.

"After the firing stopped, a man kneeled down next to me. He looked me over, then lifted the cross I was holding. He said, 'What do you know?' Tank commanders name their tanks and paint those names on their gun barrels. The name of the tank was the Celtic Cross. It had a picture of the exact same cross I was carrying painted on it.

"I found out later that the tank had been separated from its command and was speeding back toward HQ when the crew heard the explosion from us hitting the IED. If I hadn't stopped at the tent and we had left when we had been commanded to, it wouldn't have been there. We all would have been killed."

Nate leaned forward. His eyes were wet. "My point is, you heard *the voice*. It told you to go find that woman. So go get her."

I raked my hair back with my hand. "It's too late, man," I said. "I screwed up. Big-time."

To my surprise, Nate smiled. "No, you're not powerful enough to override fate. So go back and finish what you started."

"She's leaving the day after tomorrow."

"Leaving to where?"

"I don't know."

"Then you better hurry."

Chapter
Thirty-nine

With Christmas over, flights were wide open. I booked one for the next day and flew out of DAB at one thirty, then changed planes in Atlanta. The whole time I worried about Aria, but I didn't call her. I didn't dare. Chances were she'd shut me down before I even got there. But to fly all the way back to Utah, well, that had to mean some-thing.

I arrived in Salt Lake City a little after 6:00 p.m. It was snowing again. Of course it was. I got a rental car and drove directly to Aria's house.

The lights were off, and her car was gone. I looked inside her house. There was still furniture. That meant she hadn't left, right?

My next stop was the diner. I ran inside, only to be greeted by Valerie.

"Is Aria here?"

Valerie just looked at me contemptuously.

"Is she here?" I repeated.

"No."

"Do you know where she is?"

"Why would I know that?"

"Because you're friends."

"Which is why I wouldn't tell you if I did know." Her jaw tightened, and she thrust a finger at me. "I warned you about her. I warned you to leave her alone. And what did you do? You went for her throat."

"I don't have time for this. Just tell me, when's her next shift?"

She chuckled cynically. "Boy, you are some special kind of stupid. She has no more shifts. She quit. After all these years, she just quit. I don't know what you did to her, but you broke her."

My mind reeled. "Do you know if she's left town?"

"Where'd you get the idea she's leaving town?"

"She wrote that she was going back to live with her father."

Valerie's face contorted, and her eyes narrowed into angry slits. "Just when I thought I couldn't hate you more, you say something like that."

"Like what?"

She shook her head with disgust. "*Live* with her father, you say. If you really knew her, you'd know that her father took his life when she was a little girl."

I was dumbstruck.

"You stay away from her, and you stay out of here. You're not welcome. I promise, the next time I see you, there'll be hell to pay." She turned and walked away.

Valerie's news had left me speechless. The words of Aria's blog came back to me. What LBH—

what Aria—had written about going to her father suddenly made sense—horrible, tragic sense. It was all right there in front of me; I just didn't see it. She never wrote that she was going back to Minnesota, she said she was going *home*. Minnesota wasn't home.

And she had never written that she was going there to *live* with her father. She'd written that she was going to *be* with him.

When she said that she was leaving "this place" to "be with her father," she'd been talking about taking her life all along. The candle had finally gone out. What if she'd already left?

Chapter
Forty

I sped back to Aria's house as fast as I could, fishtailing as I turned the corner at her street. I jumped out of my car, ran up onto her porch, and pounded on her door. "Aria, open up! Aria!"

I stepped back and kicked the door, praying beneath my breath the whole time, *Please be okay. Please, God, let her be okay. Please.*

"Aria!"

I spotted a shovel at the far end of her porch and went over and grabbed it. I was about to put it through the window when I heard something behind me. I turned around. Aria was standing on the sidewalk looking at me.

"What are you doing with my shovel?"

I froze. "You're still here."

"What are you doing here?"

I ran down to her. "I came back for you. I was wrong. And I'm sorry. With all of my heart, I'm sorry. Please, forgive me. Please. I love you."

She looked at me for a moment, then walked up onto the porch, examined her door where I had kicked it, and unlocked and opened it. She stepped inside, then turned back.

"Are you coming?" She disappeared inside.

I hurried up the stairs after her. As I came

330

around the door, she put her arms around me. Then she pushed her lips against mine.

"What?"

"Just kiss me."

When we finally parted I said, "How can you forgive me?"

There were tears in her eyes. There were tears in both of our eyes.

"I knew you would come back."

"How did you know?"

"Sit down." We sat next to each other on the couch. She wiped her cheeks, then looked up at me. "That day, when my father told me about the edelweiss, about finding a man who brings you edelwciss, he also said, 'But remember, Aria, people make mistakes. Even a man who will find the edelweiss for you may fall. He may climb wrong peaks where nothing grows. But if his love is strong, he'll find his way back to you. If he truly loves you, he'll pick the edelweiss.' " She looked intently into my eyes. "It was you. You climbed the mountain. You came all this way with nothing more than faith and courage. You climbed the wrong places; you even fell. But in the end you came back."

For a moment I was speechless. Then I said, "But I didn't bring you edelweiss."

She looked at me, and a large, beautiful smile crossed her lips. "I am the edelweiss."

Epilogue

Six months later Aria and I were married on the beach just a few miles from my apartment. We had a ceremony in Midway as well. At the Blue Boar Inn, of course. Neither Nate nor Dale made it to that one, so, fittingly, Ray was my best man.

Nate and Dale are still arguing over whether Nate lost the bet and owes Dale a thousand dollars. If it were the other way around, Dale would have paid up. Not because he's more ethical—he's just a lot smaller.

On our wedding night I gave Aria the pendant. I hadn't known why it was so important to the universe that I buy it until I showed it to her. She examined it and looked up with a big smile. "Do you know what this is?"

"The woman at Tiffany called it the Noble Star."

She smiled. "That's another name for edelweiss."

We live in Florida now, but we still keep a foot in Midway, Utah. We go back for Swiss Days. I even ran into Lynette once. It was awkward.

We bought a small winter home just a mile from the Blue Boar. A *winter* home. Imagine that. Aria said the cold was good for me. How she talked me into that I'll never know. I am getting pretty good at skiing, though.

Dale's brother is a partner in a large Miami law firm. They tracked down Wade, Aria's ex, and had the bulk of the loan assigned to him. I paid off the rest.

I finally met Thelma, the pie goddess. She didn't look anything like I expected. With a name like Thelma I assumed she was an old, seasoned grandmother making pies before butter came in cubes. The truth was, she was a year younger than me. Of course, we didn't have wedding cake for our Midway ceremony, we had pie. Ray took home all the leftover pecan.

Believe it or not, Valerie and I are now friends. Of course we are. We have much in common. We both love the same woman. Enough to fight for her. We both also like the Eagles. The band, not the team. There's nothing profound about that, but it's something.

I've thought a lot about Aria's and my conversations at the time of my quest. I remember our first talk at the inn about the meaning of her name. I've found that there are other meanings. Aria is a form of the Greek name Arianna, which means 'very holy.' Fitting, I think. But my favorite definition is the Italian, where aria means 'air.' That is what she is to me. She is what I breathe. Maybe our names really do make us who we are.

The day of our wedding, Aria posted one last blog entry. She showed it to me.

Dear Universe,
   Thank you for everything. I'm doing just fine.
                    —LBH (Loved By Him)

Like I said in the beginning, this was the story of my jump. Sure, there were a few rough spots on the way down, but I wouldn't change a thing. We fear jumping because we fear falling. We fear being broken. But still, jump we must, because it's only in jumping that we'll ever find someone to catch us.

THE MISTLETOE INN
RECIPE CONTEST WINNER

from Cathy Austin

HOMEMADE CHOCOLATE PEANUT BUTTER FUDGE

This was my grandmother's recipe. I use a four-quart Dutch oven.

4 cups white sugar
1 cup canned evaporated milk
1 cup water
4 tablespoons cocoa
2 tablespoons light corn syrup
A pinch of salt
2 tablespoons butter, plus extra for the pan
3 heaping tablespoons peanut butter

In the Dutch oven, stir together the sugar, milk, water, cocoa, corn syrup, and salt. Cook over medium heat (do not turn heat up), stirring occasionally until it comes to a boil. Once it comes to a boil, continue cooking but DO NOT stir again. Even though you will think you need to, it's important that once it boils you do not stir. Continue cooking until it reaches soft ball stage on a candy thermometer (235°F) or until a small amount dropped in cold water forms a soft ball. Remove from heat and add the butter and peanut butter. Using a wooden spoon, stir vigorously until the fudge loses its gloss and holds its shape when dropped. Pour it into a buttered 9x13-inch pan and let it cool. Once it's cool and has firmed up, cut it into squares and taste the goodness of homemade fudge.

Center Point Large Print
600 Brooks Road / PO Box 1
Thorndike, ME 04986-0001 USA

(207) 568-3717

US & Canada:
1 800 929-9108
www.centerpointlargeprint.com

BOCA RATON PUBLIC LIBRARY, FLORIDA

3 3656 0648278 1

LARGE PRINT
Evans, Richard Paul.
The mistletoe secret

JAN   2017